LIE UNDER THE FIG TREES

A Novel By

TAD WOJNICKI

 Edward R. Smallwood, Inc.
Tucson, Arizona

Edward R. Smallwood, Inc.
Tucson, Arizona
Copyright © 1996 by Tadeusz Israel Wojnicki
All rights reserved. Published 1996
Printed in the United States of America

02 01 00 99 98 97 96   5 4 3 2 1

Thanks to the efforts of my editors, Kathleen Stanton and
Marva B. Hoffman, this book is more than just a figment
of my imagination.

Cataloging in Publication

Wojnicki, Tadeusz.
    Lie under the fig trees / by Tad Wojnicki
    p. cm.
    Preassigned LCCN: 95-071531
    ISBN: 1-881334-33-3

    I. Title.

PS3573.05653L54 1996   813'.54
                                QB195-20586

To my workshoppers, who kept me from starving
in more than one way.

Shall ye call every man his neighbor under the vine and under the fig tree.

Zechariah 3:10

Therefore I lie with her, and she with me
And in our faults by lies we flattered be.

William Shakespeare

Down deep every loser harbors high hopes. The hopes burn his sleep, fry his nerves, run him around Manhattan, a bone in his jeans. How do I know? I've harbored some myself—teach college, lie with Rosie, taste the tropics. The highest hope I harbor right now is to smuggle my angel into the U.S. over Christmas—that's in forty-eight hours.

Continental Flight 444 to Mexico City leaves at six A.M. It's 2:30. I can't sleep. The ice grains attack the window. It sounds like zillions of tiny stabs. I hope a snowdrift won't block my door.

I must get a wink before Hersh Kochanowski, the travel agent I share the studio with, gets up at four A.M. I gotta go for my pill, the best sleeping pill I know—the cocktail I came up with on another sleepless night—Smirnoff vodka and mango juice fifty-fifty. The bottles of vodka and juice stand guard on the windowsill above my futon at all times. I reach for the juice. It's frozen stiff. Nothing comes easy. Everything puts me down, even a bottle of juice. My life. My luck. I grab the Smirnoff, swill it straight.

Back in Poland, I wished to break free, live in California or another warm land where one can run around naked. One should lie "under the vine and under the fig trees," my father said, quoting the Bible as he remembered it from the little Jewish upbringing he had. I went around telling everybody.

"Under the fig trees?" my classmates ridiculed, pointing at the snow outside. "It's a dream of a cut-off head." They had a point—snowdrifts blocked our door for almost half the year. But I trusted my father. He had a way to hope things out. If they worked out you laughed to tears, if they flopped you cried to laughter.

As I see it now, my father was a *shlimazel*.

Well, my father, like my mother, like my younger brother Roman, the whole goddamned family, myself included, were all born losers. As far back as I can remember my life in Poland, we were unlucky; born losers, sons of born losers. I came from a distinguished line of *shlimazels*. We tended to screw up stuff before getting it right, if ever. We all, maybe except for mother, were *shlimazels*. I scorned us. On one hand, we blossomed with lofty ideals, on the other, we always became victims. Sorry stuff. Made me hate myself all my youth.

Beaten up by the boys, I jeered myself, "It's good for you!" and would have given myself another kick while lying on the sidewalk, if only it was possible. I held a disgust—a strong, relentless one—for myself. When I first felt liver pains, a sign my body was rejecting Polish food,

I refused to see a doctor, hoping it would develop into cancer. "Misfits like me don't even deserve to stay alive," I sneered. Sometimes, wriggling in pain in my Warsaw apartment following a meal at the graduate student eatery, I was close to giving in, calling an ambulance. The moments of weakness, I called them. "Don't touch it!" I'd snarl at myself at those times, "Let this damn fool die." I managed to never check it out. Somehow, I'm alive. Polish food didn't kill me. Only once, seeing I was dying, my ex-wife called a doctor. I didn't appreciate her saving my life. The only consolation of staying alive was the hope I'd be dying again.

Yet I yearned to lie under the fig trees and I hated the snowdrifts blocking my door. I felt damned. Why be damned? Then I recalled kids back at school calling me "The Chosen One." I thought I knew what it meant but I was scared to ask. "Are we Jewish?" I confronted my father.

"Sins of the fathers are visited on the sons until the tenth generation," he said. That's why. Goddamned us. I laughed. What else was there to do? Just laugh.

My life was full of laughter. I dreamt of teaching philosophy. I wrote a smart Ph.D. thesis, defended it successfully, got rave reviews—then, I let excerpts appear in *Die Zeitschrift für die Jüdische Geschichte*. High honor.

But the communist regime considered it anti-regime. The honor made me unemployable. Denied a teaching job, I fell to the level of an underground stock clerk at the state archives.

In the basement I dreamed of California. Every co-
dex, folio, scroll, annals, swirling with dust at a touch,
every papyrus crumbling into powder, every bookworm
hole, even every sneeze and headache—not to mention
bloodshed caused by the sharp edges of the pages—made
me crave the sunshine. I submitted a research proposal.
I said I wanted to study the Egyptian pyramids. I lied.
Passport in my hand, I hitchhiked to Paris, and flew to
New York.

In the United States, I fired out a hundred curricu-
lum vitaes to colleges all over California. A chilling "thank
you" from Paraiso Springs College followed a warm "position has been filled" from Coldwell Institute. While the
Bottomless Pit Bible College made me feel high, the High
Sierra Poly threw me into a depression. As Whispering
Pines University made me howl, Dry Creek College made
me cry. But the Orange Orchard College made me feel
just rotten: "We don't have any position suitable for you
at the present," it reported, "and we don't expect to have
any in the foreseeable future."

So instead, I laughed hard, skinned my hands washing pots at David's Delicatessen on Broadway, on the
Lower East Side, trotted drinks around the indoor pool
at the Olympic Club, froze my ass off on the concrete
floor of Royal Cannery picking crab meat, and—until last
night—torched myself by the Nirvana Pizza ovens. I'd
fallen to the bottom.

The studio I share with Hersh is in a deserted warehouse. On some Manhattan nights, no less harsh than Polish nights, the liquids freeze on my shelf. Snowdrifts block the studio door exactly the way they blocked my boyhood door. It's the lowest Lower East Side. The studio has a living room and a small vault on the way to the john. That's where my futon is. At every breakfast, I am visited by a cockroach I later see down on his luck in my coffee cup.

Lately, I've been eating mostly pizza. Cost? Zilch. I've become all bone and flab. My joints creak and my ribs started showing—I saw it the same night I saw the first pubic hair turning gray. I've been spending my days at the Renaissance Cafe, drinking coffee after coffee.

The Renaissance Cafe—the writers' and artists' joint some call "the snake pit"—jumps. It's in Slush Alley, just around the corner from my studio. I love to sit at the table under the fake ficus tree, bullshitting with Hersh, Carlo, Tip, and the other *shlimazels*, or eyeing the Dirt Cheap Travel Agency office across the alley, daydreaming, waiting for something. What for? I didn't know.

Then, around Rosh Hashanah, I was sitting there, under the fictitious ficus, my knees bouncing, fingers drumming, gawking, as usual, at the Dirt Cheap Travel window with Hersh at his computer, selling an exotic trip to a client, when I saw that huge photograph behind him—a tourist couple with drop-dead tans in a tropical paradise hiding their nakedness with a fig leaf.

Suddenly, I remembered that back in Poland, I had wanted to lie under the fig trees. What was I up to now? Rotting in the Big Apple? Baking pizza? Living like a dog? In America? How low can you fall?

Under the ficus tree, throbbing and horny, I recalled Róża Izabel Rotko, now living under martial law. Why forget her? I can't forget her—couldn't all these years. "Róża Izabel Rotko," I said. "Róża Izabel Rotko," I said again. It made me dizzy. I'll bring my angel over in forty-eight hours.

I take another swig of Smirnoff.

I'm jotting everything down, everything that's true, just for the record, before falling unconscious.

2

The Christmas before I defected from Poland for America, my wife had taken a train for Christmas Eve dinner at her mom's, carrying off our baby daughter. Barred from teaching college by the regime, I had no gift money. I stayed home, homeless.

Things were cracking up. No water, the pipes froze. No food, the shelves stood empty. The fridge was out of order. It generated heat, not cold. All my wife had left for me was a box of rye crackers. Soon, they were gone. I felt like hitting the road that night. I tapped the buttoned pocket in which I kept my documents. In fear, I opened my Polish passport, checking and re-checking every date, every stamp, every visa to make sure the Polish customs clerks found no reason to stop me, and buttoned the pocket back up. I decided to wait. I wanted to take the Ph.D. exam, set for January 17, 1977. I wanted to get my *philosophiae doctor* title, useless as I knew it would be. So I thought of food, real food. Where could I get it? Downtown, all shops were closed. The only place I could get anything to eat was the Warsaw Rail Terminal.

In the street, the worst frost I could remember. Sidewalks were empty. The wind blew snow under the chained tires of the last trucks carrying Christmas trees. The paddy wagons sped past. The undercover police kept busy picking up street girls and dissidents. Peeking into windows, I saw big dinner tables. My eyes devoured the piles of pork chops, the trays of fried fish, baskets of sweet rolls, slices of poppyseed *babka*, lumps of honeycake, the loops of *kielbasa*, pots of *bigos*, or hunter's stew.

Quite often, I saw the traditional free chair for the stranger. The chair stayed empty. I saw people eating, hugging, crying, joking, exchanging best wishes, drinking vodka, or just opening their mouths—singing carols. The kids unwrapped gifts in golden paper.

Inside the terminal, the radio said the frost made the trees' limbs crack off. There was a *meshuga* man at the counter, cracking jokes. He asked, looking around, "What's the definition of a chamber quartet?" and he answered, bursting out cackling all by himself, "The Moscow Philharmonic *after* a tour of the U.S." There had been a rush of Soviet defections at that time. The subject was taboo, though. Soon, the wisecracker left. Nobody told "Polish" jokes in Poland. What they told were "Russian" jokes, all politically off-color. Poles told them slyly, among friends they could trust. Nobody cracked them at the Warsaw Terminal, of course. It was *meshuga*. If someone did, nobody laughed.

There was a girl at the counter, writing in her school

notebook, who'd "missed" her train. I had seen her before. Then I recalled she used to be an usher at the State Jewish Theater on Grzybowski Plaza. She was a robust bumpkin, red like an apple, pretty—too pretty, actually, not to be a bit rotten. She appealed to the teacher in me. She was down, so I said, "Down deep every loser harbors high hopes." She wouldn't hear, so I said, "Know what? You ain't ugly at all."

And she said, "My Daddy never had to tie a pork chop around my neck to get the dog to play with me!" It was her pet expression, I later found out. We started talking. It turned out she was a student at Copernicus High, my neighborhood school.

The same night, she joined me within my four walls for some sweet Manischewitz wine I'd saved from a Hanukkah party a week earlier, and dried apples. I looked at her as we kissed, petted and necked, getting drunk. She was snow-skinned and snow-breasted, had a long neck and a muscle-shaped, pouting mouth that made me feel slow and soft as I'd never felt before. Love at the first fuck. Blitz. Thunderbolt. Straight stab in the heart. She wept. Nobody in Poland hurts bad compared to a girl who's "missed" her train on Christmas Eve—certainly not a Jew, hardened in his homelessness. But I felt for her. *Avodim hayinu,* I remembered my father say, "We were slaves." She touched something deep within me. We wept together.

I talked her into opening her notebook. We read it

by the candlelight. The notebook was titled "Charred Nestlings" and was filled with poems of wild hopes.

Then she walked around the apartment in my wife's slippers showing off her hourglass body. It cheered her up.

"If the headlights of the paddy wagons were cockatoos," she giggled, peeking through the frost blooms on the window, "it would feel like Mexico." For some reason, she thought Mexico was synonymous with paradise.

That's when I said I might help her make her dream come true one day. Helping a stranger may be helping an angel.

Waking up, I hear Hersh making coffee, then I see the bottle of mango juice frozen stiff on the windowsill. I recall I don't work at Nirvana Pizza tonight. First thought, work! A well-trained dog's reaction. Tonight, no work. They said they needed staff to handle the Christmas traffic. I said I must pick up a girl at the airport. "Fired!" my boss blew up. I'll deal with the unemployment when I'm back.

I'm off to Mexico City within two hours. Soon, bundled up against the worst Manhattan frost I can remember, I'll arrive at JFK Airport. No skewering by the pizza oven tonight.

It's 4 A.M. on the clock.

"Think Rosie'll leave Poland before the Soviet tanks crash through the gates of Warsaw University, Doc?" Hersh calls from the kitchen. "What's wrong with her?" he barks. "Does she think buttercups like her don't get rolled over?"

Hersh walks in, flexing his muscles above my futon. I don't feel like getting into that again. I know Hersh. Bitter. Cranky. Nasty naysayer. Wild about women as I am, but wild the bad way. I love women. I forget the bad. One good one does the trick. Rosie did it. Just like that. I'm like a newborn. But Hersh? He's a case. He divorced just recently. His ex sued him, stripping him bare. Could blow up at a moment's notice. But I feel for him. To feel is to forgive.

"Isn't there something fishy about her?" He stabs the air with his hand, pointing at Rosie's picture above my typewriter.

"What do you know?" I say. "You hit it off with someone like this only once, if ever."

"But in her letters, doesn't she stink?"

"She's young."

"You're an old dog, for Christ's sake, Doc."

"So what?"

"Why her, Doc? There's tons of blond, blue-eyed *shiksas* around waiting for a sugar daddy to put them through college."

"Recall how long I've gone bananas over the girl? Five years? Six? Isn't it crazy? Really crazy? Something to consider?"

"You've gone bananas over a mug shot, not a real girl."

"I've had the hots for the girl, the real girl, since the first night at the Warsaw Terminal."

"Cool off."

"Besides, she's a member of the Walesa family. Consider that."

"Cool off," Hersh says.

"Now?"

"The tickets? The hotels? The meals? The drinks? The rings? The earrings?" Hersh slips on his college ring. "How can a Ph.D. pizza-baker afford that?"

"It cost me zilch—"

"Besides, you'd be wise to lay aside some cash for emergencies. You were mugged at Nirvana the other night. You're danger prone, remember."

"No rings, no earrings, no *tchotchkes*, no *shmattes*," I say. "It won't be that costly."

"One thousand dollars minimum," Hersh says. "Sounds like a damn costly date. Tip warned you about blind dates, Carlo says it's plumb loco, I think it stinks. You're being hurrah-optimistic. The whole damn snake pit roared the other night when you shared your stinko, wacko, psycho plan with them."

I fall silent.

"For that cash you could get first class sex at the poshest Madison Avenue hotel."

I punch the wall.

"No sex till I get her back to New York."

Hersh throws on his jacket and grabs the door knob.

"I can see your 'no-sex' bull at work as you shlep all over Sexico by Jeep. I can see it! First, of course, you stare into each other's eyes, trying to understand what's going on; then, shyly, you hold hands; then, you pet; then, you neck; then, you wrestle; and finally, one steamy night, without knowing how or when, you roll her in your sleeping bag—all the while, of course, maintaining your 'no-sex' bull. I see it!"

The door slams and Hersh is gone. He might drop in at the Renaissance Cafe later today, but he would argue with an empty chair.

People put me down a lot. I feel down now. But that's where I've got to get to bounce back. First I hit rock bottom. Then, I go the other way—I hit the sky.

4

"Welcome aboard Continental Flight 444 to Mexico
City," Captain Youngblood booms through the loudspeakers. The luggage rattles in the overhead compart-
ments—we're taking off.

The cabin is packed. I see Latino families, Hassidic
honeymooners, and crying babies—the whole of Manhattan on the go.

Seated next to me is a bald, sagging man wearing a
Calvin Klein polo shirt. He looks like he's sitting *shiva.*
Raw slabs of his loose jowls drag down his bloodshot eye-
lids, giving him the look of a lovable, teary-eyed bulldog.

Next to the bulldog sits a cinnamony Mexican, hugging herself with meaty arms as she talks to the blonde
by her side. The two girls' teeth and skin imperfections
bespeak poor childhoods. The blonde's dark eyes look
like empty sockets against snow-white makeup meant to
plaster the warps of acne. The Mexican tucks her hands
under her arms, squeezing them to her sides. Her breasts
bulge to her double chin. She wears a T-shirt reading *The
Bottomless Pit Bible College, Rancho Mirage, California.*
The same college that denied me a teaching job in their

Bible Exegesis Department. She works there? Maybe.
Or, like me, maybe she hopes she would? The girls talk
about things back home, in Acapulco. Unbelievable how
fast they speak. They seem to attack each other with ver-
bal stabs. *"¿Cómo cruzaste al Norte?"* I want to ask. I need
to know. "How did you snake into the United States?"

John F. Kennedy Airport has disappeared, pushed
by Manhattan. Somewhere down there, I can't see exactly where, there's my Renaissance Cafe.

It's a shock, I'm hitting the sky. I can't believe this is
me doing this! But all it took was robbing my bank, buying a ticket, and claiming a seat. Ahead lie the tropics,
my Rosie, "Sexico." I feel the way I did six years ago:
The borders, the barriers, the walls, the red tape had
given way—the world seemed to be parting before me
like the Red Sea. It was happening after being told, for
years, that it was the dream of a cut-off head. Naysayers,
stuff it.

It's December 24, 1982, a Friday, but to me here,
thirty thousand feet above the land, it's a Sabbath. I'm
separated from all the stuff down there by the *tallith* of
snow striped with black highways.

I pull out Rosie's letter. The letter has been keeping
me up nights since it arrived a week ago. I've read it a
hundred times.

Thanks, thanks, thanks for your letter. You a
writer? I didn't suspect you had talent. I'm just back
from the kitchen. Now I'm writing while eating, so if

you see stains on the paper, you know why. What does Rosie like to eat? My Mummy says it's easier to clothe me than to feed me but since I buy my clothes myself, Mummy takes advantage of me (hee-hee). It's not that I pig out, only that I'm terribly picky about food, which drives my Mummy crazy: "What," she cries, "for Christ's wounds, should I cook?" Sporadically, I eat meat.

*I don't eat fish, onion, garlic, leeks, mushrooms— none of that stinky stuff. I'm not a bunny, God's my witness. So what's left? Guess! You can't. Know my mercy—*kluski, pierogi, knedle, pyzy, pączki, kopytka, *and other balls of boiled dough which Rosie simply adores!*

Occasionally, I get a sweet-tooth, and I stuff myself with sweets to nausea. Now, Teddy, you know why I refused to send you a recent photo—you don't want to have nightmares, do you?

Have I written that I've joined the ranks of the unemployed? I've been fired. I was upset, but I finally accepted the fact I've got no job. Now I take moonlight walks, sleep till noon, meet my friends, looking for a place in life.

I'm not a little angel, God's my witness. I've broken more than one heart, but it was only because they expected too much of me. I'm too young for anything. Not ready to take on the yoke of a wife.

Christmas is coming. I love it. I feel like crying

and I think of my Daddy. It was on December 13,
1981, when he died during a strike. The Walesas
joined us at the funeral. Gosh, I miss my Daddy so.
I never told anyone, only you. You know? It's my great-
est secret! Even my Mummy has no idea how much I
miss my Daddy.

"Pretty handwriting!" the man next to me says. I feel
my heart knocking against my ribs. "Who's she, your
daughter?"

"Girlfriend."

The man looks at my shorn head, the specks of white
in my black beard, and he reaches for my right hand.

"Stew," he says. "Stew Sternlicht."

"Ever heard of the Hard Rock Club pianist by the
name Sternlicht?" I ask. "Hy Sternlicht?"

"My brother," he says.

"I loved hearing him one night down in the Village.
He's dead serious—"

"Hitting the Keys?" Stew cuts in.

"Acapulco; you?"

"Acapulco, too. Why not the Keys?"

"I want to check Rosie out, and you?"

"I want to check Hy out."

"Where's Hy, in jail?" I ask.

"In the morgue."

I feel my heart in my throat. Stew's still in shock over
the phone call from the U.S. consul in Acapulco. It woke
him up last night. Hy's body, with multiple stab wounds,

was found two hundred meters from his Jeep, under the fig trees in Ixtapa, in the State of Guerrero. Hy traveled with a girl. Reportedly she saw nothing.

Outside, the Florida Keys appear. Stew's raw eyelids well up with the Gulf.

5

"Ladies and Gentlemen, the Captain has signaled our approach to Mexico City."

Stew gave me a sneak preview, sort of, of what might be. The lump in my throat makes it hard for me to swallow. The hurrah-optimism went *pffft*.

I feel like checking out the Mexico City Air Terminal, buying a return ticket, and flying back. I have my studio, I could get back my pizza job, in time, who knows, get a professorship in philosophy, and everything would work out just dandy. Sounds reasonable.

"Cool off," Hersh said. "You're danger prone, remember," he added, referring to the robbery during my shift at Nirvana Pizza the other night.

A masked guy with a knife in his hand had walked in. "Cash," he said. "No," I said. He jumped, trying to stick his knife between my ribs. I stuck a straight left in his kisser. He hit the hissing oven behind him, got to his feet, and fled. Hersh's always right. Why risk? Rosie might like to fly back, too. Where we're both headed, one can be sure of nothing. But then, when was the last time I was reasonable?

"It's almost noon down there, isn't it?" Stew says,

pointing through the window.

"We should arrive at 10:54 A.M. local time," I say. "I checked."

The window steams with my breath. I wipe it off with the sleeve of my thrift shop camel-hair, and try to catch my first glimpse of the tropics. What I see is millions of little houses engulfed in rusty haze. The city's twenty million people live mired in a stew of air and water pollution. I see palm trees, jacarandas, eucalyptus, other tropical vegetation, maybe even fig trees. There're people down there in the little houses. They cook, work, fight, enjoy a siesta, prepare for Christmas, make merry, make love, do all their own way. In their wildest dreams they don't imagine a gringo up here giving them, down there, a thought at this moment.

"What goes up must come down," my father said. Rosie dreamed of Mexico the night we met. I've always dreamt of the tropics, too. Now, I'm getting there. Go back, now? Now, when the dream is coming true?

The moment the landing is announced, some passengers rush to use the bathroom before the belt-up light comes on. So does the girl with the meaty arms. I climb over Stew's knees. I point at my chest and say my name.

"Teddy," she repeats, smiling. "*Muy bonito.*"

I point at her.

"Epiphany," she says.

"Funny for short?"

She nods, laughing. Her black eyes flash from under

her thick, grown-together eyebrows. The Latin women are said to sprinkle orange juice into their eyes to make them sparkle. Funny doesn't need that. Her peepers flash like Times Square at midnight.

"*¿Cómo atravesaste la Frontera?*" I whisper. "How did you slither over the border?"

"You want?" Funny asks, pointing at my belly.

"My love wants."

Epiphany bursts out giggling.

"*Rápido*," she says. "Fast!"

"What to watch for?"

"The *coyotes!*"

Where to cross the border? At what time? Who're the *coyotes?* A million questions wire me up, but Captain Youngblood booms to sit down and belt up.

"I heard you say you lived in Acapulco."

"You like?"

"I'd like to see you in Acapulco," I say. "I don't know anyone there."

"Gimme a buzz."

As she is writing her telephone number, I discover the big secret behind her arm-wrapping: Her nails are chipped, many of them broken and, it seems, permanently black. Her fingertips have saurian callouses. That's why she keeps them out of sight. I figure she, like me, is a professor who, exactly like me—being a fresh immigrant—works with her hands, greasing heavy machinery.

"I'm coming to Acapulco with a girlfriend."

Funny gasps. She looks at my naked, pushy head, then at my beard, and smiles. *"Las canas no quitan ganas,"* she says. "Just because you've got gray hair doesn't mean you don't have desire."

I burst out laughing.

"Is she jealous?" Funny asks.

"Yes."

"Poco veneno no mata," she says, giggling. "A tad of poison won't kill."

From what I understand, Funny came to the United States as an illegal and she is legal now. She sounds like a terrific source of information. Best, she doesn't mind sharing it.

"See you in Acapulco," I say.

At the Mexico City Air Terminal, Poland is front page news. I catch a headline: "Arrests Among Opposition in Warsaw." Hersh would've asked, "Is your buttercup among the jailbirds, Doc?"

I buy the newspaper, look for Rosie Rotko, but don't find her among the arrested. I check the list of those killed by the police. She's not among the dead.

I hope Rosie gets the hell out before the tanks roar onto the Warsaw University campus. It gives me creeps just to think about it. I study the newspaper picture showing demonstrators huddling, kissing, waving signs, screaming demands for human rights. It's been boiling under the surface since the military crackdown last December. The lid's finally blown as the first anniversary of the crackdown came; the Polish police and military are getting more and more brutal. Then I imagine the tanks crashing into the crowd. I see Rosie, looking like a goddess with blood-gold hair and voluptuous golden eyes, being rolled over. I shudder.

The picture is blurred but I can tell exactly where it has been taken. I recognize the Humanities Department, where my Ph.D. exam took place. Watching the protests against Soviet totalitarianism today, I'm sure the building recalls the protests against Tsarist despotism a century ago. I recognize a few faces of my former classmates, now most likely assistant professors. My angel's nowhere to be seen. Great, but the tanks may roll onto her campus any moment.

With its location at the crossroads between the East and the West, Poland will always be rolled over by tanks. Someone will always try to control her lands, and the Poles, feisty and stiff-necked as they are, will keep breeding grassroots heroes—Tadeusz Kosciuszko and Berek Joselewicz in the 18th century, the insurgents of the 19th century, or Lech Walesa of today—to lead them to independence.

Because of that, Rosie, who's from a family of Solidarity activists, may well find herself at any time "under a bit of 'pressure,'" to quote my roommate.

Before I leave the airport lobby, I smell the street. It's the smell of a building in New York I watched being brought down with a huge wrecking ball. I saw the floor stains, the dampness patches, the sink molds, the bathroom mildew, the john fungi disappearing in a cumulus of toxic dust. That's what Mexico City smells like.

Now I step outside and stop dead. I've just entered a blast furnace. I can't breathe. I can't move. The airport lobby was air-conditioned. There was no forewarning. Funny, I flew thousands of miles away from one oven only to find myself inside another. I go from oven to oven.

I fight my way past taxi drivers assuming every gringo is a Baron Rothschild, and I take a metro. The Linea 1 connects the airport with my stop, Chapultepec Park.

7

The Hotel Excelsior blooms like a nipple on the brick-brown square. Children run screaming in and out of the open-air lobby. They're tanned, fun, and they wear Made-in-USA T-shirts saying *I Gotta Have It* and *Just Do It*. One cherubic boy is called Pancho, possibly after the 19th-century bandit hero Pancho Villa. A guitarist carols "Stille Nacht, Heilige Nacht" in Spanish:

Noche de paz, noche de amor!
Todo duerme en derredor ...

"Señor Teddy?" the receptionist asks. It takes me a few seconds to figure out that he really means me. The way he says it sounds like "Tevye," my Hebrew name. I had no idea how the Mexican mind would change my name. But maybe I had no idea how the Mexican mind would change my mind, either.

I nod. The receptionist hands me a letter. It's addressed: "Teddy, Hotel Excelsior, Mexico City." No return address. I recognize the scent. It's from Rosie. My heart is doing crazy jumps.

"Corona," I say at the bar, sitting on a stool and tearing the envelope open.

I'm sitting at the bus stop, a damn bus driver didn't stop to pick me up, they're awful, goddamn goons, these bus drivers, God's my witness. It's snowing, the holes of my shoes are filling with slush. I don't know whether you'll be able to decode these scrawls because my hand got stiff and all I got is this stub.

When was it written? Date? None. Place? None, as usual. There's never any information on when or where she writes. Drives me mad, but why? What do I want? Did she ever take a paleontology, historiography or methodology class? God forbid. What for? One hair-splitter mind between the two of us is enough already.

But dating her letter now, just days before her defection, when every second counts, wouldn't be asking too much. It'd help our communication. How sweet it would've been for me right now—at the Hotel Excelsior bar—to know when the letter was written. No such luck. All I have is a crude notebook page, the kind I still remember from my school years, reeking of Poison perfume:

My reservation is for December 22, but I'm in a mess. Everything's screwed up, though in this particular case it's not my fault. Everything's stretching like chewing gum (it's shaking 'cuz in the meantime I got on a bus.) I'd love to take advantage of my short visit to Mexico and do some research while there. Getting off.

She's not coming for "a short visit," of course. Nor "to do some research." It's to fool the censor. The truth lies between the lines. She's coming to this hemisphere to stay.

Staying here is not just "staying here." It means—Hersh is right—being together all the time, peeling her Levi's off, stripping naked before a shower, dropping her soiled panties in the laundry basket—all that.

She knows that her "staying" here is all that and more, and that sooner or later—rather sooner than later—we'll end up sharing not only the coffee cup, the typewriter, the bookshelf, the clothesline, the phone, the john, but also the futon. Even before that—Hersh is right again—we'll take off in a Jeep and shlep up the Pacific coast, sharing my sleeping bag.

And what's her reaction? None. It drives me nuts. No reaction is a reaction, of course. Why doesn't she at least mention her resolve to stay with me under one roof, though? Why? *Not* because that damn censor was going to poke his nose into the letter. She couldn't care less. *Not* because she's being skittish. She's not skittish. Far from it. Why, then?

God, of course! She takes it all for granted! For her, going out with a man could mean only one thing—counting the stars over his shoulder. For Rosie, it's all natural, all normal, all the typical order of things. Sure thing. *Sine qua non.* Something to look for. Something to expect. Something everybody does. Something we did, too, the first night back in Warsaw. For her, it's simple: We shlep together, we sleep together. It drives me nuts, God's my witness.

The desk clerk calls a maid, a giggling girl with a braid of golden-brown hair as thick as a *challah*, and I follow her upstairs into a squeaky hall.

The maid keeps giggling but it's strange; she makes no sound, gagging herself with her hands. She just shakes all over. Is the giggle a lie? Is it a sob? I don't know. Name a lie, any lie, and I have probably gone for it. Gullible? Me? Well, yes. I'm a fool that way. Only when she takes a bill I offer do I see her lips, stretched ear to ear and her tongue like a red pepper, flipped up.

The room is dark. I smell the dust, tobacco, and rotten fruit. The vaulted ceiling makes it a cell. I remember ceilings like this from the medieval convents I saw in Poland. Plush curtains block the high noon sunlight. The bathroom blinds are broken and light blazes through the slots, burning holes in an antique bathtub. The good thing is the light comes in from two directions—from the garden and the street.

First I check the bathroom window escape. I always do that. Why? Don't know. Pogrom survival instinct, I guess. The mold and mildew around the shower curtain need scrubbing. In the tub, a big cockroach scrapes the glaze trying to steal away. It's fine with me if we stay under one roof, but will it be fine with Rosie? I doubt it. I crush the cockroach with my shoe and flush it down the john. Feels bad now. Like snaking a buddy. Why did I do it? I climb the rim of the bathtub. Right under the window there's a busy street with its gear-grinding, honking, vrooming, dust-swirling, fumes-belching traffic.

The houses across the street are nouveau-riche. The most striking features of this architecture are the wrought iron bars, fancy grillwork and spikes. The work takes the shape of hearts, doves, praying hands, crosses, and holy figures—befitting a Catholic nation. Through the beautiful metalwork the hungry can see luxury cars parked in the driveways and watch family clans pigging out on terraces beneath arbors of bougainvilleas, vines and roses.

The walls dividing the villas from the street are blank and tall, the kind that are damn hard to scale, and their ridges are jagged with broken glass set in cement. The glass seems to come chiefly from champagne and beer bottles. The shards protect *la vida dulce* inside. I despise the way the rich keep it to themselves, but I can't help admiring their fondness for the finer things in life.

Above nouveau-riche row, I see the Latin-American Tower. Seeing this Empire State Building lookalike makes me feel at home and I go to check the opposite window.

I feel more and more like this is a nunnery. There are holy pictures of La Virgen on every wall. She's shown holding baby Jesus, her heart bleeding. Rays grow from her heart, looking like spikes. The drapes block the sunlight. I push aside the heavy, hot fabric and a golden dust boils in the dark. I open the window on the riot, cacophony and collage of a walled garden.

The gnarled branches of a giant fig tree reach the sill. They make it possible for a strong man to climb to our room from the garden. I sniff the sickening, sweet smell of rotten fruit, the blooming, the fetor of earthworms. I suck in all.

The tree is arthritic, ancient, welcoming. Writing my dissertation, I came across a funny bit of information. The tree of knowledge was really a fig tree, *ficus sicomorus*, not an apple tree. To taste its fruit was to taste the flesh and fluid of God. This tree hosts so many birds, bats, bees, bumblebees, flies, butterflies, mosquitoes, and God knows who else—all buzzing, humming, chirping, screeching, peeping, whizzing, cooing, whooping—that it sounds like an orchestra tuning their instruments before a summer concert in Central Park. I shall taste God soon.

Beneath the fig tree flourishes a tangle of flowers. The snapdragons, phlox and lady's-mantle crowd the roses—all wild for attention.

In a banana plant I spot a couple of banana rats nursing their young. Against the wall kids play hopscotch, raising hell at every mistake a rival makes.

The mahogany bed is big, solid, with a fat baby angel,

or *putto*, as my high school fine arts teacher called it, sculpted in bas-relief on the headboard. I lay down. The bed is pretty hard, the way I like it.

What am I going to do when Rosie arrives? First, I'll invite her to have a bite, hopefully not at an airport restaurant where they'd skin me alive. Then, I'm going to take a taxi back to the hotel. Can't shlep her in the metro. Gotta impress her, at least this first day. Economizing starts tomorrow. Then? What then? It worries me what kind of a date this's going to turn out to be.

In New York it seems I only kept in touch with women I knew from high school. I dated them in art galleries. First, I saw a bunch of Rubens beauties. Rubens insisted on an overall plumpness, and for a while it was perfect. Then I visited the wenches by Renoir I always loved. I stayed at the Guggenheim Museum at times till it closed, horny, hungry, thirsty, eager and paining in more than just one way, trying to figure out whether it was true what contemporary critic Alfred Wolff said, that Renoir painted his girls as if their flesh was putrefying. Then I dated Gainsborough's and Watteau's girls. Like John Keats, Gainsborough insisted on a waif-like anemia but after a while I realized I liked them because they reminded me of my ex-wife, and I quit seeing them. I discovered a sex shop at Times Square.

But there was a woman I knew back in Poland who I saw in New York only in dreams—Rosie. It happened especially when loneliness was driving me nuts, that means quite often. It was a shame I couldn't recall her face, though—just her red-gold hair, her lewd golden eyes and hourglass body, after all these years.

Now I want to get this body back close. I want to rev my system with bare skin to bare skin, the down against the down, breaking into sweat, getting clammy, with her neck wet to my lips under long hair reeking of a sappy shampoo or her Poison perfume, stinky now, badly over-heated, her skin slick, snow-white, smooth to my face, then rough, goosebumped, and then slick again.

Quit driving yourself up the wall. Things are on the up-swing. If you sin, at least enjoy it, I think, falling uncon-scious.

• • •

An eighteen-wheeler roars down the street. It sounds as if it's dying. I jump off the bed, climb the bathtub. The rig is gone. A short hot shower hisses on the asphalt. Sidewalks are empty.

Across the street, the rich smile in their *casitas,* sip-ping refreshing fruit drinks tinkling with ice cubes on the terraces under their multi-colored umbrellas.

The sunshine is gone. The sky is black. I watch the thunderheads stabbing at the Latin-American Tower. I can't believe the weather. It changes so fast, sweet God. It's Mexico. It's the tropics. I feel like jogging down the street in my birthday suit, *Whoopee!*

9

I don't know a city until I get it in my feet. I walked Paris from Belleville to Boulogne, New York from the Washington Bridge to Battery Park, and San Francisco from Embarcadero up to Twin Peaks, all in 1977. That's how you get to know a place—the life sounds, the stone texture, the taste of the food, the aromas of its coffees. And among these the most telling is the shape, the smell and the taste of bread.

It's only noon, I still have two and a half hours before I have to be back at the airport, so I decide to get Mexico City in my feet. Outside, the freshly scrubbed red-brick sidewalk blinds me like a steaming mirror facing the sun.

The first great thing I notice is a noisy market right around the corner. People carry out fruit, fighting cocks and pottery. Dogs tear the garbage to bits for scraps of food, driving the sewer rats nuts. The dogs fight, bark and growl. Urchins throw stones, and when one hits, dogs howl, then yelp. They act like wild coyotes. They are skinny, scabby. If the Mexicans' bellies are full, their dogs' bellies are empty. Nobody loves them. The Mexican dogs fear people.

Nearby in a niche there is a cross. I experience *déjà vu*. The Christ is disfigured by arthritis or paralysis, sprinkled with blood, has rathole wounds, and a head of thorns—exactly as portrayed in Poland. Creed of pain. Who suffers most, wins. People kneel, lay roses, light candles. A young woman slaps her kids down to their knees. Their black, sparkless eyes look up at the Christ, learning how to wound.

Paseo de la Reforma is my next *déjà vu*. I feel I'm back in Paris. The boulevard was copied by the Emperor Maximilian after the Champs Elysées.

Walking la Reforma I reach Chapultepec Park. I stop dead at the statue of Tlaloc, Aztec god of rain. The huge rock monolith—weighing 165 tons, I recall reading in a Dirt Cheap Travel brochure—had lain for centuries on its back at the bottom of a wild mountain gorge near Texcoco. A violent storm broke out the day the rain god arrived in Mexico City.

Another shower hisses on the pavement. I hide under the trees. One minute later, the sun explodes again, and the god is steaming from the shower.

I reach another traffic circle and another *déjà vu*—a winged girl shoots a thin but triumphant arm above the trees on a Corinthian column, like the Nike at the Place de la Bastille in Paris.

"What monument is it?" I ask a man who looks like the god Tlaloc, wearing an Indian poncho.

"El Angel," he says, wobbling away.

The population of Mexico City is twenty million—
the descendants of Olmecs, Toltecs, Aztecs, and the *con-
quistadores*, all mixed up. They show up in person to greet
me dressed in Indian garb, workman's overalls, business
suits, chic gowns, or beggar's tatters. I love the pale sports
suits men wear. I sweat like a horse in my camel-hair
coat. There's a sea of heads I've seen nowhere else in the
world, only here, carved in rock ages ago. The sea of heads
doesn't part. Pushed, shoved, bumped into, I fall from
the curb, in danger of being hit by the soot-belching lem-
ons whipped by yahoos.

There is plenty of food but I cannot eat it. The meats
are sizzling in the smoke of taco stalls. Can't just walk
by. I watch the fat drip, sputter, scream in the fire. Foods
are fried, deep fried, hardened, darkened, burnt, full of
lard or animal-fat drippings like back in Poland. I'd forgotten that for most people these foods are a delicacy as
they were to me long ago and far away. I can't believe it
now that I keep kosher. My belly flattens against my spine.
The food still smells great but it is unclean. The meats,
especially the beef, seem to have come from animals who
died a violent death—far from kosher.

I stop at a hole-in-the-wall *tortillería* to watch a pretty
girl mold the dough on a stone slab. I love the way she
shapes the pies. Nirvana Pizza would hire her on the spot
to handle the Christmas traffic.

"*Disfrútalo*," the girl says, offering a tortilla that feels
like a matzo. She winks, then giggles. I love this people.

I offer cash but she says no, seeing how I sweat in the noon heat. I feel that I'm wearing too much cologne. Maybe I had hunger in my eyes. I bite into the tortilla. I like the muggy smell of it; this corn matzo must be the local bread, I guess.

That's when I see a department store. The hotdog dummies look skyward, showing off. I step in, fit into a sand-hued sports suit, and throw my New York rags in the trash. Trash returns to trash. I don't miss my thrift store elegance. The only piece I keep is a white T-shirt bearing the blood-red word *Solidarność*.

You can easily spot me in the crowd—I'm the white-clad baldhead with a black beard. That's the way I dress from now on—white slacks, white jacket, blood-red logo shirt. "Why should a pizza-baker wish to wear white like a medical doctor?" I hear my roommate ask. "To show off splotches of tomato sauce, black olives, and sausage grease? It's just not practical—it shows dirt, Doc!" I defy that kind of thinking—I wear white *because* it shows dirt. I like clean clothes. But the dirt is there, it's everywhere. If I get dirty, I get dirty. If there's dirt there I want to know there's dirt there. I won't ever again wear black to avoid seeing what's there.

I pass giant display windows flexing my muscles. My muscles ache for exercise under the flabbiness caused by too much pizza. I stride, my hands deep in my pockets, my shorn head trying to outshine the sun. I remind myself of my father, his stride and—if I recall well—my father's father's stride. My grandpa had the same stiff, brief, purposeful stride. I like it that I walk the way they walked. And I like the play of the light and shadow on my legs. The play makes me think of the halls of my high school, lined with copies of classic sculptures. The way the light shaped draped bodies always amazed me. I have never stopped watching what the light does to a shape in motion—like my calves now—pulsating inside the white fabric as I fling my feet.

I enter the Zona Rosa's streets, named after world metropolises. Makes me feel at home to see the names of the cities I've got in my feet, and I say it out loud and as I say it I see this city's face is flushed.

Finally, I see Calle Varsovia, named for the city I thought I'd escaped forever, here in the New World.

And in Warsaw Street, just off Reforma, I see a cafe much like my Renaissance Cafe, named El Coyote Flaco, maybe for the looks of the average patron, the goddamned *shlimazel*. The stench of marijuana pinches the eyes. "*El pinche gobierno*," the graffiti reads, "The fucking government." Like the Renaissance Cafe, this cafe is not a high-paced, spinning world. It's a pit of doggone hopes, a bottomless pit.

That's where I'm sitting now after the walk—seconds before leaving for the air terminal—knees bouncing, fingers drumming, nodding toward the empty chair, and writing to you.

The Mexico City Air Terminal is madhouse. For a moment, I think of my father and the way he wasted away in a psychiatric asylum I would never know, and whether he ever stopped thinking that one day he'd lie under the fig trees. But I'm him now. This thought makes the madhouse my home.

With the T-shirt screaming *Solidarność* across my chest I'm a walking billboard. I want Rosie to spot me right away.

I flex my pectorals to give the word some play. It seems I've developed some muscle bulk since this very morning. The pectorals under the blood-red Solidarity logo feel like two bulges. The harsh lights shine on my head.

I check it in every mirror. Will Rosie like me now, six years later? Will she mind the hair I lost as the result of my pizza diet? My skin's early aging in the heat of the ovens? The crow's-feet from too much laughter? But maybe her daddy was a baldhead, too? Bet he was—big, slick, oily globe for a head just like me? Maybe. He grew no beard, though. He wasn't a rabbi, that's for sure.

Aeroflot Flight 114 from Havana has already landed, the loudspeakers say.

Where's the plane? Where's the gate? I jostle through the crowd, looking for information. I spot the arrivals table; Gate 52. I push for the gate, throwing furtive glances at my reflection in the windows of the boutiques.

I find the exit, *salida* in Spanish. There's only one blonde in sight. Not Rosie.

I watch my shoes shooting forward, talk to myself, offer greetings, hallos, bye-byes, smiles, whisper sweet nothings, foresee Rosie's reactions, mimick my responses. I try them out on some girls who walk by. They first react as though I were talking to them—to them personally, not a girl who may be just a figment of my imagination, but then they quickly figure out I must be a nobody-home.

"*¡Coco loco!*" a girl says to her companions, and they dive into the crowd, giggling.

As the first hour of waiting wears on, I go from tense—sucking on a Havana cigar and soda—to playful, at one point punctuating my own steps with a loud, "Go, man, go!" and stabbing the air with my arm for emphasis. People stare at me as if I'm loco. In New York, no one would pay attention. Here, I lose face like that. I get such a kick out of it that I go on, repeating, "Go, man, go! Go, man, go!" and kissing the air.

Aeroflot Flight 114 has already landed, Gate 52, the arrivals screen still reads.

"*Pan z Polski?*" I hear a girlish voice say. The words come to me in a strange, forgotten language of my past life; it's been six years since I spoke any Polish. Phonetically, the words sound like "*Pahn spall-skey.*" Slowly, their meaning becomes clear, "Are you from Poland?"

I look up and see a tall, handsome man, obviously a weight-lifter. I see myself in a dark-haired, brown-faced, black-eyed crowd when here in front of my eyes I have a six-foot body-builder with long, sandy-blond hair. He laughs easily and asks his "*Pahn spall-skey?*" over and over again. It's a shock—from the heap of gnarled muscles comes the sweetest voice one can imagine, "Are you from Poland?"

"How did you know?"

He stabs at my chest with a powerful arm. "Long live Solidarity!" he yells. A gold crucifix dangles between the pectorals of his 54-inch chest like a coin between two pigs.

"God."

"Surprise!"

"Total."

"Gotta split," he says. "You're the first fellow from Poland I've met in years and years."

"Mountains can't meet, but men can," I say. "What are you up to here?"

"Making movies," he says. "I'm a stuntman. What are you up to here?"

"Just flew down from New York."

"Stay with me."

"There's two of us."

"Where's your wife?" he says, looking around.

"Just flew in," I say. I point out toward the crowd spilling from the *salida* following customs clearance.

"From New York?"

"From Warsaw."

"You guys both stay with me."

"We stay at the Hotel Excelsior."

"Gotta get back on location at the Olympic Stadium before two," he says, turning to trot.

"It's two."

"Gotta split."

"Teddy," I say, offering my hand.

"Like Teddy Kennedy? Teddy Kollek? Teddy Roosevelt?" He laughs easily. "They all call me Polo," he says, crushing my hand.

"So long," I say.

"Here's my card," the mystery beefcake says, handing me a card, and getting into the trot. The card reads, *Polo the Stuntman*.

"Thanks a bunch," I say.

"Bring your wife over for a drink tonight," Polo throws over his shoulder, diving into a gang of kibitzers.

11

A peroxided blonde blocks the exit, bent under a buff-colored bag, mobbed by black-robed Jesuits. Her hair, outlandish among the Aztec heads, strikes me as even more outlandish because it's curly. Is it Rosie? My angel? My hope? She looks like Rosie, especially those golden eyes, those lush lips, but that hair? That horrible hairdo? Curly mop? Tasteless wig? This girl looks like a lion sporting a new perm—an overcooked one. She keeps blowing the corkscrews out of her eyes.

She's wearing a cheap rabbit-fur coat. The fur looks bad here, in Mexico City. I'm sorry for her, for the rabbits.

She's standing there, unsure of what to do. The Jesuits walk around her. She's confused. Does she want to back out? I panic. I'm running toward her, I realize. I have no idea when I jumped forward. I only know I'm running. *Here's my fate*, it hits me. Funny, that's the only thought I have. Coco loco, honest.

She smiles, blood-red lipstick stands out in her haggard, frost-harsh face. Now I'm dead sure—it's the sunburst smile I knew. Just seeing this smile makes it all worth it. Not for the moment—it makes it all worth it til the end of time.

Tripping on her bag, knee-weak, Rosie falls against *Solidarność*. It's a hug, sort of. She's just reeled into my arms, dead tired, that's all. "Here's my fate, here's my fate," my mind rattles. I grab her bag, lock it between my legs, squeeze it with my calves in case a thief's been watching, ready to take advantage of our euphoria, and I give her another hug, a bear hug this time.

"Finally," she mumbles, squeezed too hard. I've never taken into consideration that she might say the first word.

"Yes, finally," I mumble.

"You look very distinguished," she exclaims, bending backwards. "Distinguished" is a euphemism for "old," so I laugh. What else is there to do? I gotta face it. But I didn't expect her to do all the talking. Not so fast, anyway. Everything turns out to be different than expected.

"You look great," I say, staring at her eyes, dense as honey, chalky makeup and cannibal lipstick. I don't mind at all. I kiss her. Now her lipstick looks worse. I care even less. "Really great," I add, but the hug makes me hot, my voice breaks, and I squeak like a boy.

"Great?" Rosie says, looking up at my eyes. "Having flown for twenty-four hours? Having visited Brezhnev? Fidel Castro? Having crossed seven seas?"

"You do."

"My daddy never had to tie a pork chop 'round my neck to get the dog to play with me, you know!"

We burst out laughing. I hear the same raspy giggle I remember from Warsaw. For Rosie, it's the first laughter here, in Mexico, and I'm happy for her. Things look rosy now.

"You're the same bad girl you were six years ago."

"Only more so."

"How come?"

"Gotta see."

Rosie may be a tiny bit on the crazy side, true. But the way I met her was on the crazy side, too. Spent only one night with her, long time ago. It's as if I've never met her. You know what one-night stands are like. All I know of her is from her letters, from what she writes. And you know how reliable that could be. "Words serve to hide thoughts," Rosie wrote once. I've bought a pig in a poke.

Rosie looks into my eyes, askance a bit, I can't tell why, maybe to check if I would blink, then looks down. We think looking down when spoken to is disrespectful, while the Mexicans think it disrespectful to stare into the eyes. Unaware of it, Rosie is culturally correct—she lowers her eyes. Sheepishly, I think at first. I'm wrong. She's not lowering her eyes, much less sheepishly. She sizes me up on the gut level, why not say the nut level. Is my fly open? I look down, too. Coco loco, again!

Rosie sees a gringo couple sleeping against the wall, their backpacks strapped to their wrists.

"How come they sleep standing?"

"They sunbathed bare, I guess."

Rosie giggles.

"Let's do that, too."

"You'll jump out of your rabbits tomorrow," I say. "Eat something?"

"I'm thirsty."

"How about a drink at the cocktail bar?" I say, stepping inside the airport bar while Rosie, saying nothing, drags her feet behind me.

I told Hersh I wouldn't wine her and dine her, but I'm loco about this girl, so I couldn't care less what anyone thinks. Particularly Hersh, the naysayer.

The great thing about the bar is the decor—jungle plants and flowers and two cockatoos raising hell in a cage. Someone taught them to screech, "Rotten Robbie!" and they go on and on, repeating, "Rotten Robbie! Rotten Robbie!" but, oddly, I hear, "Rotten Rosie!" Otherwise, it's a bummer. Dammit, Hersh was right, it turns out.

The drinks arrive in large glasses filled with thick slush. A radish twisted into a rosebud straddles the rim crusted with the frozen salt.

"Waiter, there's a rose in my drink!" I say once he's out of earshot.

"What?"

"Don't you like the little red radish roses dressing up the drinks?"

Rosie shrugs.

First, Rosie doesn't have the slightest idea what it

costs. She thinks this posh watering hole is one of her Warsaw student hangouts. Second, she hates the tequila. The first time she's ever had it. The waiter brings her a Coca-Cola, her drink of choice. She drinks it straight from the bottle, at times pushing the tip of her tongue down the neck. Can't show off much if your date doesn't appreciate either the ambiance, or the finesse of tequila—she just sits there, hunched in her chair, dipping her tongue in the bottle neck, ignoring it all. *La mujer insatisfecha*, I think, unappreciative woman, unaware of what you do for her. Is that who Rosie is? I'm not even sure she's aware of the cockatoos, their stubborn mud-slinging.

"How did you say it?" I say. " 'If the paddy wagons were cockatoos it would feel like Mexico?'"

"Who, me?"

"That night."

"I don't remember saying anything like that."

"It's been years!"

"Six?"

"Exactly six years tonight," I say. "That night, six years ago, also was Friday."

"Believe it?" Rosie says, rasping.

"Hard."

"You better."

"The night was terribly cold, I remember."

"Was it? I don't remember. I remember you walking nervously around your apartment, mumbling something about your upcoming doctoral exam, and repeating, 'Stuff yourself with hope and you'll go nutty as a fruitcake.' I laughed to tears!"

"I didn't say that."

" 'Stuff yourself with hope and you will go nutty as a fruitcake,' that's what you said, over and over. I thought you went nuts."

"I couldn't have possibly said that," I say. "Doesn't sound like me at all."

"I remember."

"You sure?"

"As though it was yesterday."

"Wasn't it someone else?"

"*You* were someone else."

Rosie is biting on a corkscrew of hair. I watch her lips, thinking of what she just said. I find her lips amazing. They felt on the meaty side back then but now, parched and raw, they look like little skinned muscles showing under the lipstick first lifted by my own lips and then by the bottle.

"You through?" I ask.

She gets up. No word. She just gets up and grabs her bag. I wrench it from her grip. Polish women are strange. For years, I was happy knowing no Polish woman. I may be back to the old stuff.

When the waiter hands me the bill, sixty-six thousand pesos, I feel I've been robbed. Is it the last time, though? Not if I keep wining and dining her. Once, that's fine. I tried to get the goo-goo eyes. Tomorrow, peso-pinching starts—no posh bars, no gourmet restaurants, no ritzy hotels. Just fruit, fruit, and fruit, dirt cheap here. Only now I remember the bottle of vodka in the hotel room.

"Hotel Excelsior," I throw at the taxi driver.

The rattletrap taxi drops us off at the potters' stalls. Rosie and I walk to the hotel past the Tree-of-Life statues, birds, whistles, other oven-fired goods. I point out to her two figurines, both naked except for two fig leaves. Freshly made, the clay is still wet.

"Adam and Eve?"

"Sweethearts, huh?"

"Why do they clash against each other?"

"The figures are bookends," I say. "They should hold a brick the size of *De Revolutionibus Orbium Coelestium* between them." My joke falls in a heap before Rosie's wan smile.

We enter the hotel.

"Wwwowww," Rosie says upstairs. "Is this our room?" She is excited for the first time.

"Pretty snazzy, huh?"

"What does 'snazzy' mean?" my celestial being snaps back, speaking fast. Her voice makes me think of the Nirvana Pizza punch clock back in New York.

"Oh, you know, jazzy, zazzy, pizzazzy, fancy-shmancy—that sort of stuff."

"What tongue is it?"

"It's English."

"English? Don't tell me that!" Rosie snaps back. "Doesn't sound like English at all."

"God's my witness."

"Don't mix God with lies."

"Honest."

I'm taken aback. Why? That's the way she was the first time I met her. I forgot it all. I forgot what she was really like, that she wasn't an angel. She was never an angel. God, never. The day I met her she was sixteen, plump, and tomboy tough. Today she is every bit the way she was then, "only more so"—to use her own words— because six years have passed. She's grown older. That's real. But not in my head. There, the opposite process had occurred. Over the years, in my mind, Rosie was growing younger and younger, prettier and prettier, plumper and plumper, more and more girlish, finally becoming a baby girl, a Rubenesque *putto*, and even—coco loco!—growing baby wings.

"Talk to me in English," she says. "I gotta practice the language before I enter America."

"This is America."

"How come?"

"This is Mexico, and Mexico is America."

"I meant the United States," she says. "What is the United States really like?"

"I can read what I want. I can watch what I want. I

can say what I want—there're no limits set for oneself except those of one's own."

"The folks?"

"Beautiful."

"I wish I could become one of them."

"I promised you that."

"Be born again."

"I promised you that," I say. "I promised you Mexico City, Acapulco, the United States, no problem. We'll get there. Tomorrow, we'll jeep off to Acapulco to watch the guys jump off the cliff, and then head straight for the U.S. border."

"When?"

"On Christmas Day."

"Hurry up. What's the date?"

"Twenty-fourth."

"Twenty-fourth? Are you sure? I left Warsaw on the twenty-fourth, been in the air for twenty-four hours plus, and it's still the same day?"

"You flew with the sun."

Rosie enters the bathroom but not to check the window view.

"I've never stayed in a hotel in my life," her voice echoes. It does to me what a punch clock does to the time card. "Look, someone left behind a hair-drier, here by the tub—" I can't make out anything else. Rosie turns on the hair-drier, a real blaster.

"It belongs to the hotel," I yell back into the

bathroom door. "You can use it as long as you stay here."

"Don't tell me that!" she yells back.

The siesta light shivers, slipping from the bed to the floor. I look up at where it burns through the leaves, and then back down.

"Aren't you tired? Wouldn't you like to lie down for a little bit?"

"Not now."

"You suffer from jet lag, without knowing it. You gotta rest. Gotta lie down for a little while and get a tiny bit of rest—then we'll walk back to the market and halve a watermelon, peel a juicy orange, split a mango, mush some grapes, and gulp a quart of fresh papaya juice! You haven't gotten any of those vitamins back home. Your taste buds quivering yet?"

The hair-drier clicks off. "Don't tell me this!" Rosie says, louder than is needed.

"Why?"

"You've promised me coconuts, remember."

"You'll get coconuts. The fruit fellow will grab his machete, slash a coconut head, and we'll sip the milk through a straw. Get some rest."

"No bed now."

"No headache?"

"Nothing."

"We're headed for the market then," I say. "Then we're going to visit a film celebrity."

"I don't want to see anyone," Rosie bursts out in

mock cries. "Only you, no one else."

"You'll love him."

She walks out from the bathroom and plops into the puddle of afternoon light on the floor. She's wearing her new T-shirt reading *Big Apple*, and strawberry-red tights. Great diet.

"I'm thirsty. Why am I so thirsty? Haven't had any salty fish on the plane, or anything—"

"You're dehydrated."

"You sweat like a horse in Mexico, huh?" she says, huffing and puffing for effect.

"Let's have a drink," I say, producing the bottle of Smirnoff and two glasses. Rosie giggles, hanging out her tongue.

I fill her glass.

"*Na zdrowie!*" she calls. "To your health!" Rosie brings her glass to her extended lower lip and gulp!—pours it all down the hatch.

"*L'hayyim!*" I call, and do the same, feeling the alcohol eating its way down my stomach and thinking how long it's been since I drank the way Rosie just did—a most refreshing sight. I cut a wedge of a mango.

"A bite?"

"It tastes slightly acidic," Rosie states, milling the wedge in her mouth, and gesturing at the ceiling with her empty glass.

"Now for the second leg," I say, recalling a Polish drinking joke and filling her glass again, then my own.

Turning the bottoms up, we laugh our heads off.

"I have to excuse myself for a second now," Rosie says, hanging her tongue out as though she were already feeling giddy, and heading for the bathroom again. Steam billows out of the shower door. "Can't think straight!" she yells back from the cloud.

I lie down, fold my arms under my head, look at the fig tree in the window, and listen to the buzzing of the insects, the cooing and chirping of the birds, the barking of the dogs, the crying of a baby downstairs. I nosh on the mango, saliva sluicing wildly around my mouth.

The bathroom sounds overpower the outside sounds. First it's the sound of running hot water, then the blowing of her nose. Then the muffled thud of a bowel movement, the squirt in the toilet bowl, the brushing of teeth, the gurgling in the throat, and finally the splash, foaming, and the bubbling of water mixed with toothpaste spit in the sink—married life sounds.

Yet another thing I was damn sure I left behind forever.

13

We enter the food market and walk past the stalls. The smells attack me from all sides—the feisty stench of freshly disemboweled bulls, the anemic breath of pork, the pungent tang of newly butchered, plucked and drawn chickens; the cold smell of the gutted saltwater fish, hugged by blocks of ice; the odor of fruits and vegetables, the hot steam of cooking, and the reek of rotting refuse.

Two lobster-faced gringos drag two gringas to a chili stall. One of them, a firehead wearing a Red Sox hat, holds a pimple-chinned girl by the elbow. She's an anorexic blonde of about thirty, wearing a T-shirt reading *I'm With Stupid*. The other, a hairy, husky, balding man with mustache, pins a brunette girl to the counter with his potbelly. He holds a foaming beer bottle in a hand like a catcher's mitt above his slipping sombrero.

"C'mon, baby, no shit," the sombrero yells at the brunette, and then turns to the stallkeeper. "Got chili in that pot, señor?"

"Noooo," the brunette screams at the ceiling rafters.

I look at Rosie. She looks back, dismayed. I look away.

The cook, sweat-faced, dips his three-foot ladle into

the cauldron, stirs his chili, looks up, and laughs at the sombrero man. Heedless of his girl's screams, the man screams right back at her face, "Señor got some hot stuff there, see?"

"*Chili con carne, señor*," the cook's wife interjects, stressing each word in beautiful, almost theatrical Spanish. "*Es la comida nacional mexicana.*"

Red Sox winks at the cook's wife but she turns away from him to kiss a baby swinging in a hammock behind her. He mimicks to the cook he wants to sample the chili. The cook hands it to him in a spoon. Still holding his girl with one hand, Red Sox cautiously stretches his neck and his pouting mouth towards the smoking spoon.

"You woke up chilled this morn, baby," the sombrero man says to his brunette. "That's what you said, 'chilled,' remember?" His potbelly presses on. He downs his beer in short swigs. His Adam's apple, the size of a potato, pumps up and down. "You gotta try this, baby," he says to her, "You gotta, you gotta, y'know?"

The brunette, the counter edge cutting deep into her soft flesh, yells back, "*Carne*? What's that!"

The sombrero man pours the last gulp of his beer straight down, his tongue looks like a giant strawberry. He throws the bottle, basketball style, in a dumpster. The Mexicans watch the lob, hoping the bottle won't crash. *Crash!*

All the gringos cheer.

"You woke up chilled, right?" the sombrero man says

to his brunette. " 'Chilled,' you said, right?" he says, winking again to the chili-con-carne lady. "Yes or no?" The
lady blushes and looks at her baby.

"Ooooawwwooooo...," howls Red Sox, who has just
downed the spoonful. His mouth wide open, he jumps
back from the cauldron. Blinded by tears, he bumps into
Rosie, stepping on her toe. The pimple-face mouths
"Sorry" to Rosie for him.

I grab Rosie by the elbow, motioning her toward the
exit. She won't go now. She wants to watch—watch my
shame, for what it's worth.

"Chase it with beer, dork," pimple-face yells at her
blinded man, pushing a foaming beer bottle down his
throat. "Or it'll blow the roof off your mouth," she adds.
She is free now. The chili took the power from his grip on
her elbow.

"See?" the brunette says to her man. "See?"

"Gonna fire you up, baby!" the sombrero says.

"Too hot, Mort!"

"You said you were chilled this morning, right?
Chilled. You said that. You said that, right? Yes or no?"

"Weee-wowww-weee!" yelps the firehead, wiping his
tears with his Red Sox hat while the Mexicans burst out
laughing in their stalls. The cook, wiping his face with an
edge of his apron, stretches a new steaming spoon to the
anorexic.

"Too hot!" she yells at the cook, waving her hand over
her mouth, then shouting, "No! No! No!"

"They think the hotter the better," the brunette says to her, pointing out the Mexicans. "The Mexican stomach loves extremes."

"Hotter is not better," the firehead cuts in, still crying. "Gotta get just the right heat to unclog your sinuses."

The sombrero man screams as he gobbles the sample pimple-face refused. He gulps some beer, yahooes, and gulps more beer. The cook stirs the chili in the cauldron with his ladle, laughing and crying at the same time.

"*Cuatro* bowls of red, *por favor!*" the hairy man says to the cook. Then he turns to his brunette and the other couple. He laughs a belly-laugh. "You guys'll love it."

They sit down to eat.

Rosie and I walk to the drinks section, buy a couple bottles of Vittel, and drink it without a word. Walking out of the food market, we can hear the yahoos way behind.

"Is that what Americans are like?" Rosie asks.

14

We enter the silverwares section. The black-velvet walls and tables are decked with sparkling plates, trays, rings, earrings and other stuff, but no real jewelry. We are dogged by stallkeepers who dart and ply us with the shlock. Rosie loves it.

"Look," she says, jabbing her finger at a pair of heart-shaped earrings. "Look."

"What?"

"Sweethearts, huh?"

"*Tchotchkes.*"

Rosie walks along, a small gang of young, quick, eager kibitzers in her wake. Part of her charm is her clunky platform shoes. Sporting her strawberry tights, my squeeze looks berry good. She has got a helluva good body with good boobs. "*Esos melocotónes son enormes!*" I overhear a kibitzer drivel, "Those peaches are enormous." Rosie throws her head from side to side. Always moving, her peroxided hair makes a swirl of tufts and quiffs in front of my nose now.

I help her through the crowd, nudging her a bit this way or that way. There's electricity in her flesh. Nothing's changed since that Christmas Eve back in Warsaw. It'd be sweet to lie down now, have her stare at the convent's ceiling over my shoulder. Stop pumping yourself up, I tell myself. There's time for everything. The excitement will wear her out, the jet lag will hit her, and she'll have to get some sleep. And there's only one bed—she saw it. If not the jet lag, the day'll end no matter what and sometime tonight, sooner or later, thou shalt lie with her. She knows that. We shlep together, we sleep together.

We dive into what seems to be a clothing cave. Mountains of merchandise in all colors pile on the tables left and right, burden the posts, and hang in bunches from the rafters overhead. First there are cycle jackets, mostly Made in Hong Kong or Made in USA, and girlish dresses, flimsy and see-through, spinning slowly in the wind one can only imagine. Rosie goes from one thing to another, checking, touching, stroking—especially a bright green jacket lettered *Monkees* and another, nail-studded black leather, reading *Hard-On Work-Shop*, made in San Francisco, California. She goes from item to item, getting the feel of everything. She shows no signs of slowing down.

"How do you feel?" I ask.

"With my fingers," she says.

"I'm serious."

"I'm serious, too."

"Aren't you running out of steam, angel? Be honest."

"One moment I may collapse and you may have to carry me back to the room—in your own arms! You're macho, aren't you? I'm the weaker sex, you know."

"Say when."

"You think I'm light, perhaps immaterial. The angel for the Christmas tree, sort of. Sounds like it, y'know? I'm not, if you want me to tell you the truth, not a lie."

"It's a joke."

"God's my witness."

"Say it's a joke."

"See sometimes."

"I'd love to."

"Don't be shocked."

The sun bursts down from among the hanging clothes, smashing against the piles of T-shirts, the sellers' faces, their hands, hopes, lighting the sweaty faces of their wives and the naked bellies of sleeping babies. Men in white hats walk up and down the narrow passageway, jostling, thrashing, wheeling, getting in halfway, stopping and moving on, pushing in and out.

Rosie stops, touching a green dress.

"You'd look good in that dress," I whisper into her hair, which is glued to her neck with sweat.

"That mold-hued one?"

"Don't you like it?"

"Don't you like my clothes?"

"I do."

"This dress, for example," she says, laying a meadow-flower print against her body, cupping her breasts with her palms, sliding her hands down her torso, and pulling her tummy in flat against her spine. "I have one like this."

"I remember."

"You do?"

"You wore the dress at the Warsaw Terminal that Christmas Eve I met you."

"So you don't have the mental sclerosis I was scared to death you had."

My hands shake but then I think, *Why spoil things? She's just a foul-mouthed kid.* My anger goes away.

"You also had a picture taken in the dress, remember?" I say. "I keep the picture on the wall above my typewriter."

"Don't tell me!"

"You'll type a letter to your Mummy on that typewriter in two days."

"Wanna see it."

"It's there."

"The flowers look great on me, don't they?"

I spin her in my hands. The electricity gets so vicious that my hands start shaking again.

"The flowers look good on you but to me you would look much better on the flowers."

"That's news to me."

Leaving the clothes market I see an Indian girl sitting by wicker baskets of red peppers. The peppers look like dog penises. The girl is reading a picture romance, a red bloom running high up her cheeks.

"*¡Socorro!*" a man howls, "Help!"

I throw two thousand pesos into his hat.

"Feed the poor until they bite your ass," a black man says, walking by with his girlfriend.

"What's wrong with an act of kindness?" I say, laughing.

"The pesos you gave him was zilch. More generous of you was to let the thieves who keep watching us, mark the target," he says, walking away. "Careful now."

It's true, I gave the beggar a deep look at my stash. No traveller's checks, just cash. I feel a shiver run up and down my spine.

"What did the Yank say?" Rosie asks in Polish as the black couple walk away.

I tell her.

"Be careful now."

"That's what he said."

Hotel Excelsior's rosy walls loom above a stall when I see a vendor, his arms outstretched, rushing up to Rosie.

"¡Bonitos!" he sings. "Beautiful ones!"

He holds some ugly silver earrings against Rosie's cheek while she strikes a pose, blinking her eyes at me. The small gang of her attendants cheer.

"Sweethearts, huh?"

I have to do it. Sooner or later, I have to do it. I told Hersh I'd buy no rings, no earrings, no *tchotchkes* or *shmattes* in Mexico. So I feel guilty. Should I feel guilty? "If you got to sin," my papa said, "at least have fun."

I grab Rosie's hand and drag her, shoes clunking, hair

flying, everybody laughing, to see the vendor's collection. Ten grand? Fifty? One hundred? What'll the robbery be? Whatever it is, I'll pay. That's it. The vendor sweeps the mud in front of us with his gestures, winking like crazy to his partners-in-crime, laughing their heads off. The moment you decide to do it, you pay no attention to what a joke you're making of yourself. All you do is stare at the crowd, the Excelsior Hotel above the pottery stall, and the empty dresses circling in the late afternoon breeze bringing the stink of the salty fish, the smell of the disemboweled bulls and the reek of the scraps torn by the hungry dogs.

I walk out past the potter's stall with the happiest woman in the world hanging on my neck. The vendors harass us with a double zeal. "Fuck off," I say left and right, "Fuck off."

"Where're the Adam and Eve figurines?" she asks, jabbing her finger at the empty space left by the bookends. "Where have they ended up?"

"In the oven."

"What for?"

"To get fired."

15

"It's time to juice up my life a bit," Rosie says, stabbing her finger at what looks like the potter's grandchild breast-feeding her baby. The mother is in Levi's, while her baby, no older than two, is in full fig—the lace dress makes it look like a wedding cake.

"Let's go mango, huh?" I say, nudging Rosie toward the fruit market, but she still stands in place, watching the mother feed her baby. She can't get enough of them.

"Girl here wouldn't be caught dead without a baby," Rosie says.

"They carry 'em, feed 'em, overfeed 'em, punish 'em, caress 'em, dress 'em as wedding cakes, readying 'em to get married and repeat it all over again."

"The mothers love their *niños*," Rosie says. "The *niños* climb them, burden them, slap them, pee on them, bite their breasts, yet they keep bringing them ..."

"Into this pit."

"Right."

The potter's granddaughter squints her eyes as the baby pats her face with its hands.

"No love is selfless," I say. "The mothers love to be loved."

"Everybody does."

"The more *niños*, the more love, they figure."

"Start early, too."

"Have you noticed, too? Babies have babies. How about you? Ever dreamed of a doll of your own patting your face with its little hands?"

"First I want to know the taste of life, not the taste of a nappie," Rosie says. "Didn't you get my letter at the hotel?"

"Sure."

"What's on your mind?" Rosie says. "Wish you could taste a wedding cake?"

"I already have."

"No kidding."

"I told you."

"You never did."

"The night my ex took a train for Christmas Eve dinner at her mother's."

"Can't recall."

"I told you I had a daughter."

"No kidding," Rosie says. "Where's she?"

"Where she used to be, somewhere in Warsaw."

"Do you write to each other?"

"My letters come back."

"If I should ever go back to Warsaw, I'll find her, I'll find her no matter what," Rosie says. "How old is she?"

"Twelve."

I'm losing my memory, it must be the heat. The heat does not keep me from noticing things, though. Without a baby, a woman here thinks of herself as not respectable. A baby is her credit card. No woman leaves home without it. They walk around, yoked with baby bundles. They don't mind the yoke.

All women imitate La Virgen de Guadalupe. They all want to be Virgin-Mothers. Their babies, like the baby Jesus, gives them a proof of the immaculate conception—of never having been laid. The only way to get respect from men.

That's why Mexican girls very early dream of having a baby. The desire to have a *niño* is an early sign of wanting sex but being ashamed of it.

Does Rosie want a wedding cake? She wrote she doesn't. I wouldn't be surprised if it turned out to be a lie.

16

Everything, every color, every line, every light and shadow is sharp as a machete. It's like stepping into another world, which it is. The world is loco, intoxicating. I walk past the heaps of rotting refuse. The foods have been lying under the open sky since morning—the first time I walked by—crawling with flies, and mixed with the earth itself, the lovely dirt.

"*¡Papayas! ¡Guayabas! ¡Aguacates!*" a girl shrieks into my ear. She must be one of those walking fruit vendors. She stuns me. I didn't see her at all.

I stagger on, feeling all tingly, drunk with love for being here. Rosie steps at my side, her platform shoes clunking, pecking my cheek from time to time—but not just pecking my cheek. At one crowded stall, standing behind Rosie, I feel her palm on my zipper. My cock jumps to stab her palm, and she grabs it. If I felt free taking off from JFK Airport this morning, I feel totally free here right now.

"*¡Papayas! ¡Guayabas! ¡Aguacates!*" I hear the Indian girl again. Judging by her voice, the girl is approaching us with her fruit tray.

The girl looks like a mountain of footballs wrapped in human skin the color of a brown bag. At first I don't see her face, she comes with the sun. I see the coconut-sized lumps of fat, piled up one on top of another, and all wrapped in a school uniform—the cocos of her hips, her breasts, her thick elbows, her lard-padded shoulders, with the ball of her head wedged between them. Rosie says something in Spanish, the vendor girl turns to her. Her buttocks look like two cocos grinding against each other. And only now I see that the girl's face is wrought by a tragic sadness.

The girl was probably carrying her fruit tray all over the market. She has sold almost all the fruit pieces. She has only the watermelon left. The watermelon comes in half-moons, standing in a puddle of a multi-fruit juice.

"*¿Si?*" she asks.

"*¡Si!*" Rosie says.

The girl reaches for one of the half-moons. Her hand is dark brown but her fingers are bleached white by the juices. She lifts the dripping half-moon by its hard green edge and gives it to Rosie. Then she reaches for another one, gives it me, I pay, and we sink our teeth into the red flesh.

It's hard to describe what a piece of watermelon tastes like in the baking heat of a Mexican market. The fruit's juice explodes in my mouth, hitting the roof of my mouth, churning around my teeth, my gums, my tongue. I can feel the subtle flesh's granular consistency, the friction against the insides of my cheeks but at the same time another sensation hits me, overwhelming my mouth— the sensation of bliss born from something liquid over my tongue.

The fruit is not cold, which surprises me. It's not even room temperature—it's downright warm, mild, lazy, and it gives out the overripe smell of a sweaty siesta. But it's a wet, juicy smell. I smell water, the wetness of sugary flesh that bleeds pink all over my hands, dripping from my mouth, chin, fingers onto my T-shirt, my shoes. I don't care. I love it. Can't believe the taste of a watermelon in the oven of a Mexican day when you're starved, lean, keen, wiry, and you're just about to make love. You feel it's coming, coming big, about to burst, and you feel starved in more than one way.

Now my mouth is full of the pink flesh, my hands are red, and my Solidarity T-shirt is messy. Rosie looks at me, giggling. I'm like a baby, true, a big baby, but I couldn't care less. Why should I? Who's there to tell me what to feel? I feel fruity, weightless, hollow, shitless, alive. Totally alive. Feeling alive is knowing where your hand is, where your leg is, where your head is, where each part of your body is, without looking. My mouth fills with the watermelon, my shoes fill with my feet, my pants fill with my bone, my T-shirt bulges with my pecs, my beard is soaked with the juice, and I love this market and Mexico and myself.

I've never thought of myself that way. I've always been

puny, but here? What's going on here? I can't believe it. These eyeballs? These giggles? These come-ons? These bell-pepper tongues? Grab-ass? Mexico makes me love myself for many reasons I had no idea existed.

From the moment I put on my new sports suit, I felt a change—I'm light, flowing, set forward, free to do anything, move anytime, fly anywhere, meet anyone, love anybody, even whoever refuses to love me back. I'm full of love, unconditional love for everybody and everything— the Indian coconut girl, the oven of a day, the yelping dogs.

I don't even mind the gang of boys who follow us, doggedly keeping our company, laughing at Rosie's lips— painted wide like those of a clown—her carrot nose, dipped in the fruit juice, the blond corkscrews she blows off her eyes, the stains blooming on her *Big Apple* T-shirt, her outthrust chin. She spreads her clunky shoes wide apart to keep them from being splashed by the hot, fragrant blood squirting from the watermelon's flesh, dripping from her elbows.

17

"The hotel is as hot as a potter's oven," Rosie says upstairs. "I need a shower."

I draw the heavy, plush curtains—probably meant to keep out the heat—to the side, unlock the window and fling it open onto the fig tree. Behind my back, Rosie peels off her tights, bra, panties and T-shirt, folds them neatly, then shoves them into a drawer and slams it shut. She must be naked now. My hands are shaking. The excitement rises to my chest, my mouth gets dry. Now, stop this shit, I tell myself. Don't think sex. Don't look back. Look straight ahead.

The fig tree, smelling sweet and noisy as a beehive, stretches its leaves towards me like hand-shakes. Shielded by the leaves, but not hidden by them, grow oblong, yellow-green and reddish figs. They grow to the size of a baby's fist. I still remember their sweet, mushy, grainy pulp from Poland—always about this time each year, around Christmas, my father was able to fetch a fistful of Jezreel Valley figs, a few Jaffa oranges, a stick of cinnamon, some cloves, a lemon, maybe two, and hopefully a mango in the rare delicatessen stores. I know the taste of a fig but I've never seen them mothered by a tree.

I don't move. I just look. I am all eyes. I stand there, my head hanging on my chest, my body loose, my hands holding the window wings, and I look down under the tree. The fallen figs lie in the clouds of shit-flies mixed with shattered glass. A bottle bottom grins at the sky, shining in the dirt.

The picture of a jar of jam flashes through my mind. Miss Jenke, my Fine Arts High teacher, gave me, the weakest kid, a jar of strawberry jam. It became my obsession that day. I craved to taste it. I got so wired I couldn't concentrate on my classes. Finally, I snaked into the locker room for a taste. While licking the jar, I dropped it to the floor. I scooped the goo from the concrete into my soap-box and ate the jam between the shards for a week, maybe more. Can't believe how alive Poland comes for me here. Must be the smells in the heat that do that.

In the flowerbed under the tree, in the deepest shade, I detect a struggle. Something is going on there. First, I can't believe it is what I think it is, but as I watch for a moment, I'm sure: A snake, the size of a baseball bat, is swallowing a bird. The bird is not feathered yet, all rosy, just a nestling that had fallen from its nest. The baby bird seems to be doing well, its eyes agog, its beak agape in an expression of rapture, but its lower body is in the snake's mouth. I notice a slight spasm of my chest muscles.

Back in Poland, Wilga, the girl next door, went to get

grass in a babushka for her bunnies. There was a snake in the grass. When she took the bundle into her arms the snake bit her in the neck. But now, I can't see either the bird or the snake. As I look, a juicy fig plops like a moldy pulp into the shards.

Behind the branches, stretching their hands to me, fanning and parasoling their oblong offspring, I can see other branches, deep within the tree. Some of them are thick and gnarly, living in the shadow of the young branches.

A male pigeon is making love to a female—treading her, ornithologically speaking—on one of the branches. The branch is caked with shit, a dating spot. A rosy balloon is stuck in the tree. There's something printed on it, but I don't get it. Probably a Mexican idiom. Bees walk all over it, frustrated, mistaking it for a huge blossom. The tree is big, the figs are sweet.

Bliss is near.

I'm jolted out of my spell by the silence of the shower. When it was sprinkling steadily, I didn't hear it. I heard it only when it stopped.

The tingle of the ripe fruit and the rot of the fallen crop fill the room, vibrating with the buzz of bees, the mumble of the bumblebees, the zigzags of the wasps, the quick orbits of the flesh-flies—all wrestling, overpowering, treading the blooms, forcing their way between their petals, down into their wombs.

An arm snakes around my neck from behind, locks

on my neck. The arm is soft, smells of body lotion, and is steaming from the hot shower. I see corkscrews of steam rising from white flesh.

In the middle of my back, below my shoulder blades, I can feel a fist—a small fist, but a fist—holding the corners of a fluffy towel. The water from her hair, that bushy, curly, peroxided hair slithers down my back.

"I'm going to lie down now," I hear Rosie's whisper. "I left the perfume I like best, Poison, by the shower hoping you wished to smell sweet. Would you like to take your shower now?"

Bliss is near.

18

I lie with Rosie in my arms less than twelve hours since leaving Manhattan. It's six P.M. on the clock. I can't grasp the stuff I've packed into these twelve hours.

We curl up, our legs looped over each other's loins. The nunnery cell reeks of raw oysters—the sweet smell of success. Rosie's heart ticks like my parents' bedroom clock, and her tummy rumbles. Her lips part. She breathes through her mouth, her nose is stuffed up. The jet lag's caught up with her and she sleeps, her face crumpled, lined with streaks the color of the neighborhood sidewalks.

This part of the trip is crowned with success, I must move to the next, the real one. The problem is, I can't. Not now. I'm snake-bitten now. Hard to figure out what next. I can't stop thinking of the present. I can't sleep. I'm wired. My senses are hyped to the max.

Rosie's flesh shocks me still, white as an unbaked pizza, but I know the Mexican sunshine will soon bake it red. I'm getting used to the nakedness. Rosie is getting used to it, too. She doesn't insist I throw a sheet over our bodies. In fact, any attempt to cover her with anything drives her mad. She is sweating. Her sweat has a bite to

it. Her perfume, overheated, has turned into vinegar and
mixed with something putrid. She smells fecund. Makes
me think of Pacific fish, algae, oysters—and I love it. I
watch a pool of perspiration forming slowly in the hollow
of her throat. "The room is as hot as a potter's oven," she
argues.

But I must admit; at first, I didn't like Rosie's knees.
They are red, bulging, calloused, as though she spent every
day of martial law on her knees in her university church.
Her breasts turned out to be big—bigger than I remembered them—and her thighs heavy. Her knees, though,
looked especially bad against her doughy thighs.

Out of her tights, my squeeze looked like a lump of
pizza dough to be shaped into a human form. Her
unbaked thighs tasted berry sweet to my tongue. I ate
her ripe nipples, the back of her knees, the small of her
back, her rosebud asshole, all the time letting her squeal,
yelp, howl, whimper. I can't recall the last time I was so
loco about the vitamins. Rosie's a well-balanced diet.

The greatest shock was to discover that Rosie's peroxided perm was a wig—exactly as it looked. "Was your
head shorn? Were you arrested?" I said, looking at her
bald skull with amazement. "Wigs are my weakness," she
said, unwilling to elaborate.

Having felt her body, I see we've been made of the
same stuff. I like it now. When I fall for someone, I fall
for every part of their body, seen or unseen. Now I like
her knees, her thighs, her double-scoop boobs, every-

thing—and particularly her buns, the greatest buns in the oven. She's born for tights.

Earlier, I saw a way Rosie uses her buns. While brushing her teeth and talking to me at the bathroom door, Rosie kept the bathroom door from closing by clutching it right between her buttocks. With Rosie, the fanny is a clutching tool serving to grab anything and hold it tight.

"You've got more oomph than most young boys," Rosie whispered into my ear after we'd done it. The difference between this time and the last time was like between night and day. I should jump for joy. Hersh said once, citing the poet Julian Tuwim, "No man ever forgets the impression he made on a woman." I'm sure it's true. I'll never forget the impression I made on Rosie.

But how about the "boys?" That stabs me. Stabs me really deep. Well, I'll never forget the "boys" either. She's laid a helluva lot of them during the last six years, God's my witness. I'll have a tough time forgetting that, but now? Now, I'm the one who's got more oomph than most of them. At forty. Quite a boy.

American men don't grow up, it's said, they always remain boys. I detect those boyish, maybe childlike, traits in myself, definitely marking me a *Homo americanus*. I recall Miss Jenke saying: "All boys and girls grow up. Only poets remain children." I felt like I was a poet all my life. Once a boy, always a boy. And today I'm a bald-headed American boy lying in Mexico City's poshest fleabag with his fellow poetess.

We have made love with the window open. The chatty garden life seemed to move inside the room. Throughout the lovemaking, I had the impression that Rosie's hair buzzed with bees. I heard the pigeon cooing, the girls playing hopscotch. If I said the kids played hopscotch, I'd lie. What I heard, in truth, were girls playing hopscotch, not boys. Why do girls play hopscotch, not boys? That's how it was back in Poland.

I keep hearing the fig tree dropping its fruit, the bombs of sweetness crashing through its hard leaves, then plopping onto the path. Now, I listen as the mangos, figs and oranges fall through the hum of the wasps, bees, bumblebees, and mosquitoes.

We didn't have to keep quiet, which I love. The nunnery's walls appear to be thick—unlike the walls of new apartments, where they seem to grow ears.

The family next door is back from the pool for their siesta. There're four of them, the old folks and two boys. I can count them because they all step on a board that squeaks. Their footsteps seem so close that I panic they might knock at our door.

Both boys cry their lungs out. They're against the nap. The mother spanks them. The boys' trunks give wet claps that echo against the high ceiling of the hall. Moms here beat their kids a lot, I've noticed. I saw the mom beat her boys in front of the crucifixion off Reforma, and then again at the market. It is as though the greatest responsibility for a Mexican mother is to break her child's rebellious spirit. Has anyone here heard of *Child-Rearing and the Roots of Violence?*

After the beating the boys cry even louder but neither parent listens and soon, having dumped their toys, the boys fall asleep, and all I can hear is the parents' bed at work. Their headboard scratches against the wall right behind our headboard. The headboard is like ours, I guess, made of heavy mahogany. It sounds as though someone is chiseling a hole in the back of my own skull.

The wife speaks—a quiet, stifled voice. It must be coming from underneath a ton of male meat. It's as though she said, "Get off me," and added, "Enough already!" I couldn't make out her words. If that's what she said, it caused just the opposite effect—the chiseling got more pointed. I hear the clapping of sweaty bellies. I detect wheezing —his wheezing. A book falls with a thud from the night stand, a big book, maybe the Bible. The man slows down. There was a tone of accusation in the thud. Now, he stops. He probably picks the book up, kisses it, and puts it back on the night stand.

Their bedsprings voice what sounds like a complaint. They're back at it. But as soon as they're back at it, it's over. The man bellows into a pillow. He sounds like a slaughtered bull, death rattle and all. I strain my ears trying to hear the woman's peak, but I can't hear a thing. I hold my breath, hoping to hear at least a squeak, a sigh.

Nothing still. I take another breath, wait again. I wait for nothing. That was it. The wife's biggie didn't come.

Maybe it was a quickie, maybe just a *pffft*.

Again I can hear the dogs bark, the bees buzz, the macaws screech, the girls scream their heads off, but all I can hear from the other room is a dead silence. The woman is quiet. She might as well be dead. So unlike Rosie. When Rosie comes, the whole of Mexico knows.

The hotel walls seem thick, but it's a lie. Were the walls built so the nuns could spy on each other day and night?

19

I hear a maid jingling her keys in the hall. The big maid, I believe, the one I think entered our room to lock the window. She probably thinks keeping the window open lets in *los aires*, the evil spirits. She cares about us, I guess. Her feet move a lot of weight. The board by our door squeaks. It's more like the howl of a stoned dog than a squeak. She reaches the staircase. The staircase groans when she reaches it, stepping down. It's quiet again, only downstairs, at the lobby, Señor Xavier plays his guitar. He sings "Stille Nacht, Heilige Nacht," as he did this morning while I read Rosie's letter at the bar:

Noche de paz, noche de amor!
Todo duerme en derredor ...

I saw Señor Xavier's wife but it was just for a moment. She's not allowed at the front desk. He communicates with her by yelling into the back room. She peeked through the half-open door. She couldn't help stealing a glance when she heard a foreign accent. She's a small, puffy-faced woman with bright eyes. The brightness of her eyes came from sobbing, I realized, and the puffiness was obviously the result of a recent beating. I felt I might throw up like when I saw my father hit my mother.

The hall comes alive with the steps of a spritzy wait-ress, the one with the *challah* hairdo. I hear the froufrou of her apron. The bottles and glasses on her tray chatter like teeth. She's walking by our doors, so close I'm afraid I'll have to dive under the covers—she's made a mistake, clearly, and she is going to knock at our door with the drinks ordered by some other room.

But no, no mistake. She carries the drinks away from our door. Too bad. I'd love to have a frozen beer, to lick the bitter foam from a sweating iced bottle. But I can't. I'm short of cash, badly short. Besides, I can't stop think-ing about what I have to pay the *coyotes* at the border. The *coyotes* may want to skin me. And they will. They will see I'm a novice at smuggling girls.

Again the squeaky board. The waitress is about to step on it—she is tiptoeing right by. I'm waiting for the terrible noise. But, as she trips by, her apron rustling and her feet flying, the board is silent. It's a shock. Clearly, there is a wordless dialogue going on between me and the waitress. She walked by as Rosie and I were making love, I know. Now, she's telling me she heard everything: "I know you're lying there, listening to me walking by," she seems to be saying, "So be careful now, everything's being heard here!"

Six years ago, back in Poland, it was dangerous to be overheard but today, back in the United States or here in Mexico, it's a joke. Today, I'm free as a bird. Today, I'm not afraid. I hate an apartment, I change it. I hate a job, I quit. I hate the hamburger *chazerai*, I don't touch it. I dig the juices, the fruits, the sun, the girls. I'm a free man. I can say what I want. But I still remember when it was dangerous, only six years ago.

But for Rosie it was dangerous yesterday. She knows horrors of which I have no idea. She lived through the crash of Solidarity, martial law, the witch hunts, the trials. She's got a helluva tale to tell.

The family next door wakes up. The siesta is over. The boys, full of energy again, slam the doors, rattle their toys, kick a ball, yell to each other, keep bugging their mother about something—I can't figure out what—and finally follow their father out the door.

The mother leaves last, the grating of her key harsh in the lock. I hear them on the staircase on their way to the pool. I'm afraid the noises will wake Rosie up, but they don't. Jet lag wore her out.

My arm is numb from lying under Rosie's back. Tightening and untightening my fist I look like I'm trying to catch Rosie's heartbeat. Her hair still buzzes of bees.

I can hear the traffic through the bathroom window; sounds like waves, first rising, rising, rising to a climax, then crumbling into nothing. A huge truck is passing by. Its engine, like hundreds of mechanical horses at work, abruptly dies out. The peace is sweet. I'm grateful again for Rosie.

Suddenly, right under our shower window, the peace

turns into a gut-wrenching roar. After a few explosions under its hood—each closely chasing the other—I hear the grinding of gears, the death-rattle taking forever, hard to bear, jammed by the returning roar.

Rosie wakes up with a start and tenses up, listening. Her parched, raw lips part in fear. Her irises widen, turning her golden eyes into two black beans.

"What's that?"

"A truck."

"Sounds like a tank stuck in a snowdrift."

I'm sorry for her. *Avodim hayinu,* I recall my father say—we were slaves, *lefaro bemitzrayim*—of Pharaoh in Egypt.

"It's Mexico City."

"Only yesterday, I was at the University of Warsaw campus, bundled up like a snowman, treading in a knee-deep snowdrift, surrounded by the tanks."

"And tomorrow, you'll lie in Acapulco, wrapped in a bikini under the fig trees, watching guys jump the cliffs!"

Rosie bolts out of the bed.

"I feel all sticky," she calls from a puff of shower steam. "I feel like you've smeared egg whites all over my butt!"

The hair-drier starts working. Rosie fell for the hotel beauty tools—the hair-drier, the revolving mirrors, the melon-sized showerhead. I'll have to buy her all of those as soon as we get back to New York. But first, how do I get her over there? All I know is that we have to do it *rápido*.

"I'll be at the cafe," I call, but Rosie can't hear me. The hair-drier is a diesel truck.

I crack open the bathroom door. The door squeaks but Rosie doesn't seem to notice it. She's drying her pubic hair.

"What do you look so shocked for?" she yells.

"Come on downstairs and have a Coke."

"Be there soon."

"We'll have a bite and then go for a drink with Polo at his place."

"Who's Polo?"

"The beefcake I met at the airport."

"Aren't you afraid to talk to someone when you don't know what they're up to?"

"Don't you want to meet a landsman?"

"He may be a police informer," Rosie says. "He may report to the Polish secret service that I'm up to something illegal."

"It's not Poland, sweetheart, it's America. We can say whatever we want whenever we want to."

"I'm chicken."

"Trust me."

"Trust you? You? Are you kidding me? You've hurt yourself more than once by trusting guys you didn't know, you said."

"Polo himself is a defector, I believe."

"Great."

"I'm sure."

"Don't tell me that."

"Couldn't get much from him because he had to split for a location."

"What's his business?"

"He's a stuntman."

"A stuntman? Honest? Is that what he does for a living?"

"Besides, he's a damn good looking fellow, a true beefcake."

"How sweet."

"Wait'll you see him, he's a sweetheart."

"Maybe he can get me a role?"

"Sure."

I step downstairs in my Pierre Cardin suit, macaw-bright shirt, and cherry-hued shoes. Maybe I'm a fool to have Rosie meet Polo. But again, I must start working out connections for her. Also, contact with a compatriot may provide comfort. I only hope Polo doesn't jump her bones as soon as we show up at his door.

The chessboard terrace is empty. I walk under the Coca-Cola umbrellas overlooking the pool. A girl lies by the pool in the dying sun. It's hot.

A young hunk is climbing out of the pool, shlepping his feet. He falls on top of the girl and lies there, munching on her earlobe while she stares at the baby blue sky over his wet shoulder. Finally her knee pops between his thighs, wedges his buttocks, and forces him to lift himself. He locks her body between his palms and knees. She must have told him, "You're crushing me," or maybe, "That bald guy's watching us!" Now her knee gets even more pointed. It's in his crotch. It's stuck between his buns like the tip of Rosie's tongue in the corner of her lips. They don't talk. Like all true lovers, they don't talk, they just grab their towel and, without a word, sneak usptairs to screw up a storm.

I sit down under an umbrella, hoping for a quiet moment.

As soon as my butt hits the vinyl chair, I whip out my notebook, now titled *Mexico Megillah*, and scrawl, my eyes half-closed. Back in Fine Arts High School, I used to keep my eyes half-closed at the easel, to create distance.

It's so quiet here, so good, and I have no trouble coming back to what I thought of yesterday and I keep scrawling, totally lost. It's so good being alone, searching my memory for some residue of a long-forsaken feeling that right now, as I'm remembering it, makes me come unglued. For once, I don't feel like breaking God's windows. I feel like giving thanks for making me *me*, making my body a highly sensitive tool intercepting the slightest impulse.

It's not particularly macho to say I'm coming unglued, but I don't care. I decided I'd say whatever I damn please, as long as it's true. I can come unglued in no time if I let myself. And I'm doing it now, because I'm alone.

"Can't keep your hands off a pen, huh?"

Rosie stands above my shoulder in a new Dior blouse and Levi's. "Only yesterday, I had to warm my bra against the heater—happiness is a warm bra, you know! And today, just a second ago, I burned my navel trying to put on my jeans straight from the balcony."

"Still hot, huh?"

Rosie sits down in the sun and spreads her hands and legs wide as if grabbing a bundle.

"I'll tell you something if you swear you won't get a swelled head. Swear. Swear right now."

"I can't."

"Too bad."

"Got a swelled head already."

"True, too," Rosie says, staring at my shorn globe. Sometimes people do stare at me like that.

"So?" I ask.

Rosie leans over the table as though the Coca-Cola umbrellas were a crowd of informers.

"How come you and your ex-wife broke up? With your kissing, hugging, cuddling, touching, all that? With your taking time? How come?"

"We were stupid," I say, thinking back of things I thought I wouldn't ever think of again. "We let other people split us."

The dying rays of the sun set fire to the Latin-American Tower, looking more than ever like the Empire State Building against the eastern sky. Rosie shakes her head as if her hair had caught fire. We hold hands as the drinks arrive.

"Now we could take a cab to Polo's *casita* or sit here a little longer watching the sunset," I say. "What would you like to do?"

Rosie giggles, looking around, and then she leans over to my ear.

"I'd like to check my temperature."

"You sick, really? I'll get the thermometer from the receptionist immediately."

"You, fool."

"You mean?"

"Never mind."

"You sure you aren't running a temperature, cupcake? Honestly, tell me."

"Yes, I do," Rosie snaps back. "I'm a bitch in heat, dontcha know?"

There is a kind of woman that no book in the world
has yet dealt with. Maybe just in a song. I hear the song
everywhere we go. *"Esta mujer me va a volver loco,"* I hear
a man howl, "That woman's gonna drive me crazy." Maybe
Rosie is the kind of woman he sings of. There're books
about vamps, tramps, prudes, waifs, virgins, viragos—
what for? Read tons of the books and you won't be able
to deal with the kind of woman Rosie is. With her, you
can't show off. Can't put on false airs. Can't bull. Can't
act macho. Forget the braggadocio, too. Blow up a pink
balloon, any hue balloon, and she'll find a nail to prick it.
You end up loco. Coco loco.

"Señor Teddy?"

I look up at the receptionist holding a note. Puzzled,
I look at Rosie. She's puzzled, too. I take the piece of
paper. It's signed "Polo." The ink is purple, a color I have
hated since the moment my father told me that's the color
of ink Adolf Hitler loved.

I request the joy of your
company at 10:00 tonight

"From the movie-maker?" Rosie asks.

I try to say, 'Nice, isn't it?' but I can't. My tongue
feels as if it has swelled to twice its thickness. I still hate
the ink.

"A taxi is waiting in front of the hotel, Señor Teddy,"
the receptionist adds. I butter his palm with a two-
thousand-peso bill.

"Taxi for us?" Rosie says. "Star class, God's my witness!"

I unglue myself from the sticky vinyl.

"We're coming," I tell the receptionist, grabbing Rosie's hand and running upstairs without touching the coffee. "Tell the cabdriver to wait."

Rosie and I have a quickie, just to relax. Two bummers strike, one after another: First, the bed breaks. Screeching like two cockatoos, we screw with Rosie's buttocks clinched between the mattress and the wall, deaf to the mother singing a lullaby to the boys next door. Then, I put a pillow under Rosie's hips. The pillow blows up. Feathers burst up to the ceiling, then fall all over the room, covering the floor like snow.

When we finally run downstairs to the cab, Rosie wears the ruffled dress with polka dots I gave her. Her frizzed hair pours over her doughy shoulders, blades quivering like the stumps of a crippled angel.

"I'm horribly happy you're here," Polo says, looking into Rosie's eyes through the hair hanging over his face. He's drunk. He was drunk when we knocked at his door. A crate of tequila sat under a plastic Christmas tree.

"Me too," Rosie says, giggling. Her voice is as raspy as bark. She is drunk, too.

"Let's drink to our next meeting," Polo sings soprano. He eats the inside of Rosie's hand, fills her glass till it drips, and then licks her fingers dry.

The jovial giant appeals to Rosie a lot, I'm glad. I worried she'd keep suspecting him of being a secret agent, remain hostile toward him. I feared she might even at some point confront him about the legitimacy of his status as a political immigrant. I don't fear any longer. Disregarding the past, both Polo and Rosie seem to be looking toward a future.

They should be. They're getting along well, talking about a Poland I knew not, the landscapes I didn't care much about, the Solidarity period I missed, the holiday traditions I never kept, the Christmas Eve treats I've forgotten until today. They forget about me, exchanging wishes, singing carols, hugging and kissing. There's also only a six-year age difference between them. It makes me feel like a stranger.

Rosie and Polo started off great the moment we walked in. They kissed at first sight. They've looked at each other ever since and, after a few tequilas, they held hands. Now, Polo gives her a hug and soon, it looks like, he'll be inside her pants.

I go to pee. I see my face in the mirror. It's the face of a homeowner whose home is burning.

Back in the room, Polo is dancing around the table, carrying Rosie in his arms, knocking down bottles and glasses, and oinking in Spanish:

Noche de paz, noche de amor!
Todo duerme en derredor ...

Rosie's hair sweeps dust from Polo's TV set, highboy, crystal cabinet, painted chest, hanging *piñatas* and death masks, and some of her tufts and quiffs catch the angel hair from his fictitious Christmas tree. The tree almost falls, dragged by the angel hair. I grab it, set it back straight. Polo sees nothing. He keeps wheeling. Rosie's hair sweeps my shoes. When Polo finally tries to sit down in a folk-art chair and let Rosie go, the chair cracks like a gun shot. Polo and Rosie land on the floor legs up. We all laugh.

"Tomorrow we should see the Acapulco cliff-divers," I say, sitting down on the couch with a beer to stop the room from whirling.

Rosie freezes, or maybe I just think she does. I give

her a quick glance. I see her eyes returning to me from giving Polo a telling look.

"Tomorrow?" Rosie says.

"You forgot?"

"Why tomorrow?"

"You kidding?"

Polo sits down on the floor in his legless chair, holding a beer. He looks at me through the wet hair falling down his face. "Why tomorrow? Why not the day after tomorrow?" he says. He belches. "The *clavadistas* perform every day around sunset."

"We gotta go."

"What's the hurry?"

"We have to be at the border by the evening of December 25."

"Why so?"

"I stand the best chance to smuggle her in as the border patrol relax, celebrating Christmas."

"Don't count on that."

"Why not?"

"Dogs don't relax."

"What dogs?"

"Police dogs."

"What do you know?"

Polo pulls up a leg of his pants. A hairless scar marks a place where a large chunk of his calf is missing. "Been there," he says. "Believe me."

"I'm chicken," Rosie says.

"Dogs don't celebrate Christmas," Polo says. "Can't get past the dogs. They'll get you."

"People who need it bad enough pull it off all the time no matter what," I say.

Rosie holds her glass at her lips by sucking the air from it. Her lips look like Polish sausages through the glass.

"Christmas is the day after tomorrow," Polo says. "That means you still have two days."

Rosie grabs Polo's arm and shakes him hard.

"I told him," Rosie tells Polo. "I told him." She didn't. Maybe she thought she had.

"But we want to see Acapulco first," I say.

"Who wants to see Acapulco first?" Rosie says. "*You* want to see Acapulco first. *You* do."

"I promised you that."

"Promised me what."

"You forgot?"

"Why Acapulco?" Polo says. "There's a buncha philosophical shit for you here, in Mexico City. Can squeeze five thousand years into a single stroll."

"Age's not all."

"I always dreamed about seeing Mexico City," Rosie yells, guzzling more beer. "We haven't seen any of the city yet."

"What's so hot about it?" I say.

Rosie opens her mouth to say something but she forgot what it was.

"What's so hot? Everything's hot about it," Polo says. "You even have Ixta and Popo, the two volcanoes everybody wants to touch; they're hot, too."

"Acapulco's the top of fancies and dreams," I say. "It's the place to go, trust me."

Rosie throws her glass through the window. It breaks in the darkness. I look out. The shards catch the light of the moon watching from a banyan tree's crotch.

"I don't trust you," Rosie screams at me. She is out of it.

"Acapulco? What's there to get?" Polo says, hitting his pig-sized pectorals with his fists. "Skin cancer? Water fungus? Trash fires? Holdups? Stabbings? The storied tourist spot's not what the glossy posters promise. It's down on its luck. But maybe you gotta see for yourself."

"Gotta see."

"You're loco."

"I know."

"You'll sob."

"Stuff it."

"Loco," Rosie cuts. "That's right, loco!"

"What's the best way to drive to Acapulco?" I ask, getting up on clay feet.

"Take the *calle* from Hotel Excelsior and go straight," Polo says, stabbing the air with his arm.

"Thanks."

I help Rosie to her feet and walk her downstairs to hail a cab. In the cab I hold her tight, watching bright lights. The streets teem with folks seeking some late-night eats.

"Don't their taxis have no shock absorbers?"

"They do," I say, picking a feather from Rosie's hair. "We're them."

"Is it a feather?" she asks. "Am I feeling down? Am I? Doesn't sound like me at all, does it?"

"Hope not!"

"I'm not feeling down," Rosie says with a giggle that is half lewd and half shy. She throbs, dripping woman all over the vinyl. "Not feeling down. At all. Not down." I dig her voice, I realize. It's not one of those tired voices that go on and on, particularly in the dark. It's a charged voice, a young voice even though it's raspy. The woman in me loves the man in her. "I feel up, if anything," she says, slipping her hand between my belly and my belt. "You do, too?"

"Sure."

It's amazing how straightforward she can be. I don't know whether I like it or not. I'm too drunk to think about it now.

Oh, I almost forgot. Rosie has revealed to me another of her amazing tricks today—the glass trick. As we had drinks on the terrace, she downed her Coke, then ate the ice cubes with her fingers. After she shook the last drop of the Coca-Cola into her mouth, she talked to me through the glass, her lips inside, and finally held it to her face by the sheer power of her lungs. Later, she demonstrated the trick again at Polo's but it was not the same. Back on the terrace, surrounded by the Coca-Cola umbrellas, she wanted to be with me, with me alone— afraid of plainclothes policemen—and stealing glances to make sure her show was for an audience of one.

22

"Early morning we jeep off for the Pacific," I call into the cloud of steam. Rosie is down on all fours, sticking her two fingers into her throat to gurgle up the tequila.

I feel drunk. I feel sick, too. Maybe I feel sick rather than drunk. Like Mexico outside. There're no stars, no moon, the city lights hit a low ceiling of clouds. So it's dark, but it's rather rosy than dark. It's Mexico dark. I'm Mexico drunk. It's a whole new stab-in-the-heart kind of drunkenness. I watch the curtains balloon with the darkness.

I feel like yelling, "Cut it, Rosie, dammit!" but I realize the folks next door may be hearing our long-distance conversation and I fall silent.

"How early's early?" Rosie yells back, then I hear her push two fingers down her throat again.

"Eight o'clock."

"What? Speak up!"

"There're folks with small kids next door."

"What's that?"

"Eight o'clock."

"A bitch of sicks, isn't it?"

"May I help?"

"It's two."

"Past two," I say. "Almost three."

"You're a slave driver, you know?"

"I thought I was supposed to get you where you wished to get as fast as I knew how," I say. "Still sure you don't need my help there, Rosie?"

Gurgling is the answer.

Just as I probe all the possible meanings of the answer it gets dark outside, so fast I think at first the corks blew off. The fig tree has disappeared as if dipped in a thick tobacco smoke. The whole tree shrunk all of a sudden. It feels familiar. The summer storms back in Poland hit like that. A thunderbolt would strike a power line and the electricity would be out. "The storm caught up with us," they said. It seems like a storm is catching up with us, too.

Here the electricity didn't go out. The world outside did. The feeling is the same, comparable only to one other feeling—the sun-eclipse fear. The ashen doom. The feeling every witness of Mt. St. Helen's eruption felt, I think.

My fear lifts fast. Something else lifts it, a booming noise. The noise makes me bolt to my feet. But it's rain, the heavy rain of Tlaloc's arrival.

The sound rain makes depends on what it hits. In a shepherd's hut back in Poland, the sound of the first mad-dog onslaught of a summer storm sounded like a sharp drumbeat because it landed on a tin roof. Here, the booming is made by the raindrops hitting the umbrellas on the terrace. Now, those fat raindrops sound like overripe strawberries being smashed against the flagstones.

What fury it visits upon the fig leaves! I watch the rain crush the leaves. The leaves sway and duck. The squirts doggedly try to shoot the leaves down. The water gives gloss to the fruits and boughs in the dark, making them shine wet, but makes it impossible to see what's going on inside the tree.

Where're the bees, wasps, bumblebees that walked up and down the leaves earlier today? What shelter have they taken? Is the rain hosing them off, then drowning them in the pools? Where are the bees whirling above the blooms, the flies orbiting in all directions, the mosquitoes circling in the subtle, transparent clouds? Where're they? The pigeons? The parakeets? The macaws? Nothing can be seen. It'll be a miracle if any of them survive til tomorrow.

I go back to bed, close my eyes, and listen to Tlaloc's wrath.

"It's better with the light turned off, no?" Rosie says, lying down with me.

She grasps the switch under the lampshade. Her body arches in the light. The switch clicks. The darkness falls, blinds me to everything but the flow of her outstretched arm, bent back, and her plump hip. The doughiness burns my mind and will forever. It's like a brook of boiling milk. *The infinite flowed white from your nape to your loins*, I remember Arthur Rimbaud's words.

"It's better with the light off," Rosie rasps in the dark.

I feel her hand.

"It's better with the lights off, isn't it? Always been. Love me. Kissy, Teddy, Daddy me, it's better. Oh, I love you. Wow, I, I love. Oh, my baby. You're my baby, I love you. I can feel you inside. You're my baby, I love, love, love you. I have your baby inside, it's growing. You're alive inside of me, moving. Moving, moving, moving, so alive, so. My little baby. I'm carrying you, move. Please, do move, keep growing, keep love. Keep like this, it's coming, baby. Kissy, baby, sucky, Daddy me, Teddy boy, it's coming. I love you, baby, and now you're born, and you're sucking my *chichis*, how sweet, how sweet, it's great. If I only can uncurl my toes!"

23

In her sleep, Rosie gnaws on something, a mango maybe, if I know her, that tastes "slightly acidic" to her, and her eyeballs circle as they did at the silver market, gawking at the wares and, afterward, feeling the sweethearts dangle against her cheek; or, later this afternoon, when I saw her lie under the fig trees, ogling the mudcaked balls of sweetness. We're close. We're so close I hear her bowel sounds.

The moonlight comes in patches through holes in the blinds, torching the sheets. It's like lying in a bed of lilies.

Rosie threw her thigh, mounting me. It had been a siesta special. Her thighs, though bulky, earlier today seemed weightless. Now, I get cramps. Her arms, though coiled around my neck tightly, felt yummy. Now, I get breathless.

It's so quiet I hear my eyelashes brush against the pillow. For a moment I think I hear some music coming, it seems, from outside. What's that? The Yidl with his fiddle? I feel like laughing. It's me, wheezing. A perfect reality check. When you think you hear the revolutions of the celestial bodies, don't hold your breath. All it may be is the hair in your nose.

Her breath smells of here, of Mexico. But also of the Royal Orangery in Warsaw, the hothouse I used to visit to dream of the tropics. Hopes for a sweltering summer smolder even in the snowdrifts. A hothouse was as close as a boy in a snowbound city could come to Mexico.

It's breathing all the sick scents of flowers that did it. Chapultepec Park is full of them. She doesn't need her Poison perfume. Flowers are enough, more than enough—I can't get rid of the thought of a room with a body laid out in state. The casket, the floor, the shelves, the walls, the candlesticks were suffocating under flowers—roses, lilies, snapdragons, hundreds I can't name. The mourners brought in armful upon armful of the odors. That's when I came to scorn, hate, despise all flowers. In August, the month my brother Roman died in an accident, flowers were cheap. So no more Poison. "*Poco veneno no mata*," Funny said. "A little bit of poison won't kill." That's right, but no more Poison. Not now. Rosie tastes and smells Mexico enough.

Besides, as she holds me, her body seems to me to be a body of some other woman. It feels different somehow. I noticed it earlier tonight. Her arms don't feel like her arms. They embraced Polo, maybe that's why. They feel like a yoke now—the bulk of them, the coil of them, the heat of them. I remember my high-school sculpture project, a life-sized statue of Golem, collapsing on me.

I'd been increasing his bulk, adding glob after glob of clay to his shoulders, his pectorals, his biceps, his balls, and finally the armature snapped and he sagged against me. Remembering, I feel like laughing, but my laughter is just a thought.

The heaviest object in the world is the body of the woman you have ceased to love, the Marquis de Vauvenargues said. I wonder if I have stopped loving her. I feel forced to suppress my doubt. Basic decency requires that I don't accept the obvious.

By dawn I think I know why her body seems to me to be the body of some other woman—it's because I'm not the same man.

24

I bolt upright in the bed, certain the hotel is on fire. Soot flies all over; there's smoke in the room. But it's quiet. No feet running. The sun swells in the fig tree's crotch. Outside, someone is raking dead leaves.

I had told Rosie we'll be off at eight A.M. It's six A.M. Twenty-four hours since my JFK Airport take-off. I've packed a lifetime of experiences in a day. And the trip is not over yet.

Rosie is still asleep. I don't wake her up. She can use another thirty minutes. Suffered a bitch of sicks last night, poor thing.

Rosie is a sleepwalker. That's another thing I didn't know about her. After I'd fallen asleep, I sensed her walk around, unable to find her own place. I couldn't wake up, dreaming of a man with a machete in his hand climbing the fig tree to our window. When I finally woke up, groping for her body and finding cold sheets, I bolted to my feet, afraid she might be sick again, and jumped into the bathroom. She wasn't there. I climbed the tub. The street was dead, no movement whatsoever within the circles of light. Finally, I ran to the garden window.

There was Rosie, lying under the fig tree, moving in a shadow. What's the movement? A man? Polo maybe? The thought stabbed my heart. I couldn't move. Then I ran downstairs. She was lying down, her rabbit coat under her back. By now he—if there was any he—could have climbed the wall.

"Why're you hiding?" I asked. I took her, shaky, feverish, smeared with gunk, back to bed. She can use a few more minutes, God's my witness.

I step into my pants, looking out. Under the fig tree, the gardener piles branches, palm fronds and rotten fruit onto a crackling bonfire. The stench of burning trash rises high into the fig tree, smoking the fruit, scaring away the birds and smelling up our room.

I go downstairs, walk to the tobacco store, and buy *The New York Times*. I walk to El Coyote Flaco and sit down, still groggy, at a table under an arcade, fingered by the shadow of a palm tree. I look at the clock tower across the plaza. The hands show 7:05.

Last night's shit still boils in my head. The whole goddamn trip doesn't feel like what I had hoped. Not anymore. Not after last night. A stab leaves a hole. I don't want it, but the image of Polo's arms coiled around Rosie's naked back flashes through my mind whether I want it or not.

The counter girl has a skinny face and a baby's mouth but I see the baby mouth grow big downing cookies, pastries, and other, unfamiliar baked goods. It's hard to believe her appetite because her face is so long and skinny. She gestures to me with a steaming pot of dark coffee.

"¿Café, Señor?"

I nod, and smile. She comes over. Only now I see where all the goodies have gone—into her buttocks. She fills not only my cup but also the saucer. She doesn't smile back.

The only other gringo in this cafe is a man whose eyes I can feel on the back of my head. His glance weighs a ton. My eyes catch a pair of yellow shitkickers walking by. Looking closer, I see a red handkerchief dangling from one of the boots. Now I realize this man is the other gringo's missing half.

I don't want to eavesdrop, I want them to talk freely, but they don't want my sacrifice—they whisper. The volume of their whisper keeps growing till I can't help hearing the driller say, "Cool off. Cool off. Cool off."

Soon my knees bounce, my fingers drum, but I feel rotten all the same. Rosie and Polo clicked right at his door. They clicked like Rosie and I clicked the first night— the only thing Polo and I share. Did they lie under the fig tree? Something tells me yes, they did. Maybe I'm way off. I'm sure I'm off, way off. I tend to fashion a fork into a pitchfork.

A big truck pulls up in front of my table. The greasy smell of diesel fumes hits my nostrils. Maybe it's a moving truck, maybe a garbage truck. Whenever I see one, spewing gases through its exhaust pipe, I think of those trucks the Nazis used to gas the Jews. Some Nazi genius redesigned the trucks' exhaust pipes to let the fumes belch inside. Before the trucks reached the destination, every Jew was oven-ready.

Two men throw the back door of the truck open and duck inside. They come out carrying pig halves in their arms. They bend under the weight of the rosy-colored slabs, run down a plank to the asphalt, past my table into the shade of the arcades, and disappear inside the cafe. Soon they are back under the arcades, their arms and shoulders covered with blood and pig fat, to duck inside the truck again.

The diesel stink is unbearable. I get up and step into the blinding sunlight. I walk down the street toward the fruit market. All fruits are sexy. All fruits are kosher.

• • •

I left Rosie's warm side about an hour ago and I'm returning now with a bunch of oranges, their heady, rough breasts against my chest. I'm hugging them with my arms as though ready to breast-feed.

Suddenly it's dark and big drops of rain plop against the pavement in front of El Coyote. The meat truck is gone, so I sit down to wait out the downpour. It's blowing my mind how fast the weather changes here. It's like living through a few different seasons every hour. The rain turns the sidewalk into a mirror and I watch the clock tower upside down.

The clock's gone back. When I was leaving for the

market, it showed 7:55. Now, it shows 7:30 again. The big hand broke, fell down, and dangles now, pointing at its reflection in the flooded sidewalk.

The rain stops as suddenly as it starts. I run into the hotel lobby. Time's up. We have to leave immediately if we want to get to Acapulco in time for the show. I wonder if by now Rosie is done with her beloved tool. I crack open the door to our room and almost drop the key.

Rosie lies coiled on the floor.

"What's wrong?" I cry, running, and I stop dead, seeing the garden gunk on the windowsill.

The Jeep is a jacked-up all-terrain vehicle with oversized tires. There is no hood covering the engine. As I start it, it barks out a loud backfire. I hold the wheel and Rosie holds the map as we drive off in the rain. The traffic drags, road dirt clogs the windshield wipers, and the Jeep's bald tires skid on patches of motor oil that slick the asphalt. It's 9:15 A.M.—later than I'd ever imagined we'd be off.

As far as I'm concerned, Rosie is a perfect stranger. She might feel the same about me. She steals looks that say she sees me for the first time—and she hates what she sees. Unlike yesterday. Wonder whether we'll ever screw up a storm again.

The road snakes upward and I sense we're headed the wrong way. Off to the right I see twin peaks like the breasts of the world clothed in eternal snow. Are they the volcanoes Ixtacihuatl and Popocatepetl that Polo was talking about? If so, our direction is dead wrong.

"We don't really know each other, have you noticed?" Rosie breaks the silence. "Tell me something about yourself. Are you a homeowner?"

"No."

"Really?"

"Really."

"After so many years in America? After so many years you don't own a *casita* of your own?"

"The streets are not paved with gold."

"I'm surprised."

Rosie hits deep thoughts but she doesn't share any of them for a few switchback miles.

"So tell me," she says. "What's the house we're going to live in like?"

I burst out laughing. I feel like laughing. I've just made up my mind. I'm not going back to New York. The other night, striking a match with my frostbitten hands to light a Hanukkah candle, bundled up in my winter coat and ski cap, I had a flashback—this is like Poland! Enough's enough. No camel-hair again, I've decided. No ski cap. I want to live by the Pacific, take my clothes off, sport the Adam's suit. *Whoopee!*

"The *casita* we'll live in is hidden in the palm trees atop a hill overlooking Hollywood."

"Hollywood?"

"Yes."

"Do you work in the movies, too?"

Pissed off I may be driving the wrong road, I laugh. What else to do about the stuff I've gotten myself into? Nothing! Just laugh. Let the crow's-feet grow.

I still have the old stuff to laugh about: No wife, she left me for a defrocked Catholic priest. No child; at seven, she's been wrenched from me by a court. No brother, he killed himself in a motorcycle accident. No mother, of course, she died of grief. And no father, he wasted away in a lunatic asylum, drinking himself into the grave.

"What do you do for a living?" Rosie asks.

"Nothing."

"What do you mean, nothing?"

"Like you."

Rosie bursts out laughing. "Got fired, too?"

"Yesterday."

"I felt down for weeks after I got fired. I felt I couldn't do anything right for a time."

"Right," I say. She was able to figure me out. Who was I trying to fool? Is she a woman I can hide anything from? Was she ever? It amazes me how deeply protective I can be of my own lies, the small little lies I create to save myself. How hard I work to hide things. There's no hiding feeling down. Feeling down shows. Rosie saw it. My face shows. Downfall shows first on the face, my mother said. But all this hiding I've done was not to hide the lies from her, but from myself.

The clouds clear, the sun comes out. Rosie shoots pictures one after another. At first I was in the picture but now she just shoots the peaks.

"Take one of me," I say.

"You keep puffing yourself up," Rosie says. "You make a hero face, makes it hard for me to get an honest shot."

I feel the heat on my face. I'm driving south. I was supposed to be driving west.

I see a mudwall hut painted white with pieces of mud falling off under a tall, branched saguaro. The cactus looks like a colossal menorah with gay, bright birds for flames. Bronzed in the sun, smoked in the traffic gases, the cactus is caked with dust.

An Indian *campesino*, very dark, walks out of a deep gulch on the left with a bunch of naked kids. He is nude but for a fig leaf, and he carries a machete. I pull over, engulfing them in dust. Rosie shares candies with the kids, which they eat with the wrappings on.

"Acapulco?" I ask the Indian, stabbing the air with my arm the way Polo has shown it to me.

"Puebla," he says, imitating the stabs of my arm.

If Polo was here I'd stick that straight Manhattan left in his kisser, I'm so pissed off. The Indian moves the kids away from me. Just at this moment Polo drives by.

"Look," I yell, nudging Rosie.

"What?"

"Look who's driving by."

"Who?"

Am I losing my mind? I thought it was him. Maybe I was mistaken, after all.

"Polo's misinformation threw off my whole itinerary," I say to Rosie. "Yesterday, Christmas Eve, I planned for us Mexico City, today Acapulco, and tonight, the border. Now, it's over."

"You may have misunderstood his directions."

"Take the street in front of the hotel and go straight, he said. He even pointed his arm in this direction. What was there to be misunderstood? I did go straight."

"Which way straight?"

"Besides, you're the one holding the map."

"Which way straight?" Rosie says. "This way or that way?" She stabs the air imitating Polo.

"He fooled me."

"You fooled yourself."

"How dare he lie right to my face?"

"You misunderstood," Rosie says. "You hear what you want to hear, not what one says."

"Gotta go back," I say, gnashing my teeth.

Rosie bursts out laughing loud.

"Back to Mexico City?" she asks.

"No stop, though," I say. "We'll jeep right through, heading west for Acapulco." He who laughs last laughs the loudest.

"Why?"

"You know why."

"Why not stay at Polo's one night? Just one night? Tonight? Please?"

"Don't you recall what we're really here for? We gotta get to Acapulco tonight, watch the cliff-jumpers, then take off for Tijuana at midnight."

"Why not skip Acapulco?"

"Skip Acapulco?"

"Yes."

"Acapulco's where it's at."

"Not by Polo, my dearest, and he's been in this country forever, unlike you, who's so fresh."

"You like him, huh?"

"We got the chemistry."

"That's news to me."

"I can almost feel his delicious flesh between my teeth," Rosie says, blushing. I look at her brick-colored blush, then at her big wig with its overcooked curls.

I feel trapped with a perfect stranger. What a bummer, God. I wish it'd never happened. I wish I'd never made her come. Carlo said, "No," Tip said, "No," Hersh said, "No," yet I did it. "Naysayers, stuff it," I said. They were right. I was wrong. I hoped to go for it, enjoy myself, sow some wild corn, and bring back my "Mexico Megillah." Instead, I'll bring back a "Scroll of Screw."

Now I want the hell out of this mess. But how? I'm in her grip, and she knows it. Is there a way out? A way out without making myself look ridiculous? I resent the fact I'm here. I resent it with everything inside me. Yes, I resent my being here, my still being here, and I resent the baggage I carry. What a mess.

Rosie looks at me but I see no triumph in her eyes. Triumph would be all right. It would promise maybe a future fight, a future. Her eyes express clinical consideration.

The Jeep jolts and lurches down the ruts. It barks out another loud backfire.

26

"What was your life like back in Poland?" I say.

"Great," Rosie says.

"Great?"

"Yes," she says, "Great, but not hopeless."

"You've got a helluva tale to tell, I know."

"Don't tell me that."

I see Rosie through different eyes. First I see her honey eyes—always fresh as though she'd just stopped crying—and then her half-parted lips, looking indignant about something I don't know, or may never find out, poised to discharge a volley of abuse. The fear is strengthened by the fact that she looks askance, scowling. She seems ready to file a complaint, accuse you of abuse and injustice at all times, even at the happiest times we've had so far.

"So how did your daddy die?" I ask. "That's the thing I don't know. If it is not too painful."

"Promise you won't get a cardiac infarction upon hearing this."

"You all were Solidarity activists, right?"

"I wasn't," Rosie says.

"No?"

"But Daddy was a strike-committee member at the Warsaw Tractor Manufacturers, if you remember the factory on the outskirts of the city?"

"Sure."

"He happened to be at the factory gate when the army tanks crashed through the gate this month last year."

"What happened?"

"You know what happened."

"Tell me if you can," I say. "I'd like to know everything."

"My father was a bull of a man, you know," Rosie says. "As the steel gate fell it cut his belly from here to here ...," she lifts her T-shirt and slashes her belly from her left breast to her right thigh, "and all his bowels spilt in front of the guard booth. The other Solidarity people put Daddy into a wheelbarrow and rushed him to a hospital, but it was the day after the fair."

"I'm sorry."

"Many people have died, more that it's been reported," Rosie says. "Igor told me."

"Who's Igor?"

"Igor was my love, he worked for the Polish television."

"Still your love?"

"He's dead."

"What's with your loves?" I say. "Everybody you love dies."

"He'd reported the real death toll on live television," Rosie says. "God's my witness. A big no-no. That night, we were sitting at my usual hangout and Igor was telling me about it. Suddenly two men, undercover policemen, asked him to step outside. He was beaten black and blue, then taken to police headquarters. I followed them in a taxi to talk to the *śledczy*, the investigator. He said Igor had died, choking on his own blood."

"Been though a bunch of crap."

"Surprisingly," Rosie says. "The *śledczy* turned out to be a guy I felt I could trust."

"Trust?"

"He fell for Rosie as we talked about Igor and what a great individual Igor was," Rosie says. "He went wild over Rosie."

"Trust a *śledczy*?"

"You'd trust, too."

"No way."

"If I know you."

"'You conspire with Teddy to run away to America,' he said. He knew everything about you. 'If you want to run with the dogs you've got to lift your legs,' he said."

"Broke up with that pig before too late?"

"Tried."

"The Solidarity guys caught you *flagrante delicto*?"

"I was raped in a cellar for days before I escaped the hell out of there one stormy night like last night.

"Take it off."

"Take off what?"

"The wig."

"I was shorn."

"See your skull."

"I'm ashamed."

"Bald's funny."

"Don't tell me that."

Around us, *campesinos* walk down from the marijuana and heroin hills, carrying machetes. Girls sit in the dirt, swatting flies off the babies they hold to their boobs. Everybody's got a helluva tale to tell.

Another thing I didn't know about Rosie was that she talks to herself, like right now.

"What did you say, sweetie-pie? Couldn't hear."

"You did."

"A diesel rig just rumbled by, didn't you see?" I jab the air, pointing at the traffic. "I couldn't hear."

Engines are roaring, motorcycles vrooming, buses honking, radios blasting, yahoos howling all around us. I'm glued to the vinyl. The traffic doesn't part for me.

I remember another time I couldn't hear something. In the clinic my mother said something I didn't get. Her voice was weak. It was as if she talked to herself. "What was it?" I asked, but a nurse ordered me to step out. When I was let back in, my mother was silent forever.

"What was it, sweetie-pie?"

"I'm not a cockatoo," Rosie says. "I don't repeat myself."

She suffers jet lag, I got to consider that. Something makes me go easy with her. Do I love her? Still? It's coco loco. After the show last night? The mud on the window-sill? Being treated like a doormat? The strongest love is the love of a beaten dog.

But she has a *tsures*, too. Why wouldn't she repeat what she said? It was something that, once said, could not be taken back. So she's dogged by doubt. She wants to communicate something, yet she isn't sure she can afford it. She hates to hurt me and hates herself for it.

"I asked nicely."

"You asked nicely but you couldn't care less about what I said."

"Whatever you say, I listen."

"Don't tell me that."

Whatever it was, I would like to hear it. Her withholding drives me nuts.

"I'm wild about thoughts that shoot through your mind. Why can't you tell me what you told me? Why can't you tell me the same thing again?"

"I'm not a cockatoo, I told you."

"You're being cruel, you know?"

"Cruel. I'm cruel. I'm cruel. You're the goddamn God who refuses to hear. You're Him who insists I restate what I once stated. I'm cruel."

Rosie is not cruel, she is scared. She has fallen for Polo. She's afraid she can't rely on him. The only fool she can rely on is me. Because of it, she hates me. She hates the faces I make, she hates Acapulco, she hates everything I stand for. Reason? Fear. Hatred is the fruit of fear. Scared of the consequences, she's withholding the truth. Nothing new about Rosie, come to think of it. She hides stuff from me as she does from her own Mummy.

Rosie has fallen for Polo overnight, but has he fallen for her? Hardly. I wouldn't trust him were I her. She doesn't, but she harbors high hopes. Especially now. She saw him drive by. He's after her, she hopes.

Everything happens so fast. Fight back? Confront her? Cancel the whole border jump? Leave her at the mercy of this beefcake? That way lies little understanding but much shouting. Should I withhold my love from her? Now? I mustn't. Not now when she needs my love more than ever.

This is not the way it was meant to be. This is way off the way it was meant to be. Even Hersh wasn't able to conjure this up. Not even Tip. Not even Carlo. Just Stew, the guy I met on the plane.

"Why do you treat me like this? I'm not used to being treated like this. I'm used to being respected. I'm used to having my hands kissed, being carried in someone's arms. You force me to parrot what I said again and again—I don't feel human anymore. I feel like a goddamn bird, God's my witness. Am I really the cockatoo you think I am? I refuse to be a cockatoo. What's said is said. That's it. I'm through with it, I'm through with you."

"You suffer jet lag, sweetie-pie."

"And don't call me stupid pie!"

She bursts out sobbing. I hold her elbow. She snatches it out of my grip, shaking all over. God, I hate it. When-

ever I saw my mother cry I kept telling myself I would
never make a woman cry. That damns a man, I believe. It
did damn my father—he drank himself into the grave. I
have to do something to right the wrong. But what? I
have never learned what to do to prevent a woman from
crying. I made them all cry. But here, in Mexico, I was
dead sure for the first time I'd make a woman laugh.
Looks like I'll never learn how to make a woman laugh.

Neither will I learn, ever, what it was she said. Maybe
it was something unimportant. If it was unimportant, it
was important to know it was unimportant.

28

"Hungry?" I ask.

"Are you loco, or what?" Rosie snaps back. "In this noon heat?" These are her first words in miles. She peels her hair off of her moist neck, gasping for air.

"Thirsty?"

She growls.

"Take a swig of the Vittel, the bottle is in the bag."

"Do you want me to burn my throat? The Vittel has boiled over twelve times by now."

"Bite on a banana, here, in the newspaper."

"I want something different."

"Suck on an orange."

"You're a sucker for tropical fruit, aren't you?"

"Papaya? Kiwi? Watermelon? Mango? Guava? Mango and guava juices are big thirst quenchers. Should I pull over? Maybe I can get something. Whaddya think? Wouldya suck one up?"

"I wouldn't, I know that."

The fruits are cheap but that's not what *la mujer insatisfecha* wants. Before too long I may have to go around, begging, "*¡Socorro!*"

"You want beer."

"Shove it up your three-letters, my dear."

"So what do you want?"

"Something."

"I know what you want."

"What?"

"A smack on your three-letters."

Rosie bursts out laughing. "That too," she says. "But a bottle of Coca-Cola would do."

"Should we have a Coca-Cola, you think?"

"Yes, yes, yes."

"If yes, why not?"

"Where?"

We hit the country road and watch burros, pigs, roosters, dogs, and girls carrying loads and babies.

"Anywhere," Rosie says, looking ahead at the Mexico City skyline.

"I can stop at any of these taco stands," I say. "They always have Coke."

"No."

"Why not?"

"How are we doing on gas?"

"Why do you care about gas? We're only half a tank down."

"Let's get gas," Rosie says.

"We don't need gas."

"Don't stop at any of those dinky little taco stands," Rosie says, looking at the skyline. "Stop at a big gas station and get gas before we pass the city."

A huge road sign shows the direction to Cuernavaca, Taxco and Acapulco. How did I miss the sign before? Obviously, I depended on Rosie to point the way. There is a big Pemex station nearby also. I take the exit, join the gas line, the last in a long line of stopped vehicles.

"I have to finally change some money and get some pesos," Rosie says.

I open my wallet and she picks from it a 100,000-peso bill—the biggest I had. A shiver runs up and down my spine, despite the noon heat. That's okay. As long as she doesn't throw tantrums.

Finally the Jeep is next to the pump.

"You tank the gas," Rosie says, jumping out and kicking up dust. "I tank the Coke."

I see her walk past the building, looking for something. I motion for her to get inside. That's what she does, offering no thank-you gesture, or even a nod.

I tank the gas, pay, park the Jeep, lock the doors, and go to the bathroom. As I pass the office door, I see Rosie hunched over a desk. What is she up to? I feel like walking up to hug her from behind, kiss her, whisper a sweet word when I stop dead—Rosie slams down the phone receiver and storms out, her platform shoes raising hell. Did she see me? Who did she call? Polo? I can't tell. If she did, I came too late to see.

I enter the restroom and look at my face in the mirror, washing my hands. *No hay droga mas fuerte que el amor*, reads the graffiti on the wall, "There's no drug stronger than love." I clear my throat. In the tiny restroom it sounds harsh as the bark of a bulldog.

I see the stars. There's no way to be thick-skinned about shit like this. "We've got the chemistry," Rosie said. What chutzpah. Of course, they got "chemistry." Not only that. "Physics," too. There's no way to hide it. Love, coughing and poverty are hard to hide, they say. What they don't say is, physics is hard to hide, too. So, we're history.

I stand, looking at my face in the mirror, swallowing hard, and washing my hands for what seems like years. When I finally get out, I feel like an old man.

Mexico is hell for him who keeps kosher. In Mexico City, when I ordered a beef steak at a Zona Rosa eatery, at least I knew what meat it was, more or less. Not so outside the city. The moment we hit the country, the mystery meats began.

Every taco stand we've seen so far hasn't been much more than a mom 'n' pop establishment. Typically, it was located under an open sky, in a hole in a wall, or even under a big tree. Also typically, the stand is piled with cooked, boiled, fried, or barbequed meats of all kinds with gigantic forks, choppers, and machete-sized knives stuck into the piles, and flocks of fat flies feeding, fucking and defecating all over the site.

In another country, the piles of meat would bear a price tag with the name of the meat. Not in Mexico. Here, the stockpiled meat baffles. It remains a mystery, though not quite—next to some piles, beautifully situated as though for the best effect, are the animals' cut-off heads, some cooked, the meat partially eaten out, some yet uncooked with the bristles and hair still intact—and the eyes half-shut in a dreamy expression. Some pig heads, their loppy ears bloody from their mortal fight, actually seem to be laughing.

The simplest thing to do to stay alive and respect yourself is to eat fruit. Mexico's got them all. It's a fruit paradise. I'm a sucker for fruit, Rosie's right. I don't think I'll ever get enough. I can peel an orange for the juice, undo a grapefruit and eat it out—the meat, flesh, veins, the healthy juice and all, for the fiber, then munch on a passion fruit or stick my teeth together eating a green fig, or suck a papaya, mouthful after mouthful of juice down to its redhead stone, chew a mango, and then ask the fruit-stand *muchacho* to chop a coconut so I can swill the milk inside the cavity, all for a few stupid pesos. It's kosher.

Just before Cuernavaca, a bunch of wayside stalls appear. All sell the same blankets, Texas hats, shlock jewelry, clay pots, jugs and vases. It's the land of earthenwares, made by hand. I step hard on the brakes, giving the right of way to the cows, calves, pigs and quick-legged chicks.

I look at Rosie. The skin of her face, her arms and her legs is pink. She will get burned.

"Wanna drink?"

"Something."

The taco makers call you to their stalls. By choosing one, you betray the others, or you walk away to the fruit stalls and betray all of them, and you don't feel any better as they let you feel what they think of you.

"What fruit have you a craving for now?" I ask. "D'ya feel like munching on some bananas?"

Rosie slows down.

"Going bananas over bananas again?" she says. "I don't want those four-letters any more. I'm not a chimpanzee, my dearest."

Rosie feels like staying faithful to one of the mystery meats. We've been mostly on a fruit diet ever since she arrived, that's true. I loved it. I thought she loved it, too. She had been deprived of it. Besides, the prices are ridiculously low. I had no idea she loved beef so much. That's not what she said in her last letter.

"The fruit is beautiful," I say, pointing at the coconuts, piled up in the dirt like heads. "Do you know a less sinful food, angel?" I see I start writing the mental letters I used to write before Rosie arrived.

Without a word, she turns on her heel and strolls into the cloud of greasy steam and smoke, counting the pesos she took from my wallet at the telephone stop.

I go where she disappears in the meat fumes. The fumes are freighted with flies. A bus belches by. *Tres Estrellas de Oro*, its side reads, Three Stars of Gold. People crowd the airless transporter like Jews to Auschwitz. Rosie points her pinky at a pile of mystery meat. The stuff looks like rabbit meat—pale, slim pieces shining with hot, vomity fat. I take a shot of the stallkeeper's huge hands chopping the meat with some veggies, then scooping all with her chopper into a tortilla, and handing it to Rosie.

Rosie lifts it immediately to her mouth. I watch her lips close on the fold, embrace it, almost caress it, her teeth cutting off a big bite, and then I watch her neck swell when the mouthful pushes down her throat. She looks at me triumphantly.

"Have one, too," she says and I think that I am going to kiss lips that are not kosher.

"Enjoy," I say.

Rosie sees the *chorizos*, Mexican sausages, fizzling and sputtering in their own grease in a bent tin pan. Stuffed in a thin gut, a *chorizo* looks like a baby's leg.

"Oh, it looks like *kielbasa*," Rosie says, shaking her fists. "I want it! I want it! I want it!"

Kielbasa, the Polish sausage, is made of odds and ends of the pig, including some inner organs—the stomach, heart, lungs, matrix, kidneys, sinews, bladder—and other parts, useless otherwise, like the ears and the snout, all ground together and stuffed into a thin intestine.

Before I learned that lard made food not kosher, I thought it was the most flavorful shortening around. Now, six years since I left Poland, I look at the *chorizos* as some god-awful stuff for Rosie to want to incorporate into her beautiful body, but she shakes her fists at my face, screaming, with a chunk of a chopped veggie stuck between her teeth. The stallkeeper wraps the *chorizo*, soaked with grease, into a roll, hands it to Rosie, and she pushes one end of it immediately into her open mouth.

I pay for it.

"Teddy!" I hear Rosie, calling from behind the fruit stalls down the aisle.

I can't see her between the palm-thatched roofs, but I'm glad she's near. I worried. Thought she got lost. She went shopping for blood oranges. Up to now, I've brought armfuls of oranges, mangos, grapefruits, cantaloups—"growing boobs," as she said—to her. This time she went shopping by herself.

Rosie rushes back, a small gang of young admirers in her wake, as usual, waving two pieces of fruit the size of Wilson tennis balls. What's this? Green oranges?

The faces of the local women, stoic as stone, express horror as Rosie snakes between them, pushing aside their shopping bags. "*Una loca mas,*" I hear one woman say, "Another crazy gringa."

"Look!" Rosie shouts. "Look!" She breathes hard, her gums showing as she emerges from under the thatched roofs into the sun.

The locals look at her, trying to figure out what it's all about. Business stops.

"Finally, I've found what I missed," Rosie shouts,

shaking the balls in front of my nose. I take a step back. Her kibitzers giggle. They like her. In return, she acts for them. "See what I got?" she yells, stepping ahead, horning me with her boobs. "Remember your old country? Blooming orchards? Crates of fruit? Recognize them?" Rosie pauses for effect. "Apples! That's what I've been missing! Apples."

I take one from her hand. Wrinkled as if grilled in fire, the fruit is marked with black rot spots. It's infested with insects.

"It's hard to be tempted by one of these," I say. "God's my witness."

Rosie giggles, as does her gang.

"Take a bite! You'll love the crunch!" she begs. "Trust me. Take a bite!"

I look at the apple, feel the crowd of boys around us waiting to see what I'm going to do, and I shoot the apple back at her.

"Rot!"

The expression on Rosie's face changes from tomboy tough, giggling, into something I've never seen before—a storming death.

"You're spoiled rotten by those goddamned California oranges!" she yells, her arm stabbing at the orange stall behind my back.

"¡Señora!" I hear a voice. I see the stallkeeper, a fellow with thick white hair and rumpled trousers, extending his hand to Rosie. There is an orange in his hand. At

first, I don't realize it's a gift, but he repeats, "*¡Andale!*
¡Andale!"

I grab the fruit with a grin, gushing, "*¡Gracias, senor!*
Gracias! Gracias!" and he is reaching for another one,
gesturing for me to give it to Rosie.

"Thanks!" Rosie shouts at him. "I've had them up to
here!" Her hand slices the air and slashes her throat.

"The oranges aren't any better than the apples, but—"

"I hate oranges!" Rosie screams, throwing her arms
violently, her hair flying. "I hate them, y'know? I've always dreamed about oranges, mangos, papayas, guavas,
passion fruit—all the fruits I could never have in that
totalitarian *Gehenna* called Poland; and now, since it's
Mexico, at the very damn least I can devour tons and
tons of 'em for a few goddamn pesos, I couldn't care less,
y'know? They don't taste as I thought they should. I don't
want to eat them at all, you know? I'd rather keep dreaming about 'em the way I've done til this trip. In my dreams,
the rind is not rough like a toad's skin, the meat isn't
stringy as a goat's, and the pits are not bitter as Christ's
sponge dipped in gall! I'd rather have apples!"

We walk out down the aisle. The gang of kibitzers
stays behind. We look like two newlyweds who've broken
up, just seconds after the wedding. Our seconds may
count as months, maybe years, and the trip may count as
a lifetime. What lies ahead? That's my first thought, What
lies ahead? What lies? Some things'll never happen again.
"Growing boobs," for one thing.

What's caused her outburst? Out of the blue? Some bottled-up anger, I guess, but about what?

"Makes me bark," I say, but Rosie gives her apple a vicious bite and walks on without a word. I think about the bugs she is eating, along with the bugs' feces and eggs. I shiver.

The stallkeepers laugh into their hats. Never fight with a loud woman, that's the lesson. But the stallkeepers have figured out where the truth lies: Rosie and I are two lovers born in the same country, one of whom hates oranges while the other never cared much for apples.

31

Stumbling from village to village without road signs, we enter a *pueblo* that looks like a pile of skulls and bones, fired brick-hard in the womb of time.

"These villages turn into a dust bowl when it shines and mud soup when it rains," I say. "Like the villages back in Poland."

"Sounds like whatever's bad is back home," Rosie says. Poland is where Rosie's heart lies. "In America, I get the impression, nothing's bad—American shit doesn't stink!"

There appears a motel with a pool under the palm trees. I hear screaming and splashing.

"I need a dip," Rosie says.

I pull into the parking lot.

"I need a bikini."

"Got the dough?"

Rosie shakes her purse in the air.

"I'll be back," she says.

I jump into the deep end to cool off, then lie by the pool in the stink of a nearby grill. The pool resembles a cauldron of molten gold. The breeze twists the fronds to the point they croak and squeal.

I look at the reflection of my face in the pool. The face I see is broken, off-center, the face I'd never seen before—the snout of a beaten cur. I can't believe it, but I see it, I see it. My first reaction is to deny what I see, get rid of the truth at once. How? By making what Rosie calls a hero face, by puffing myself up and, by doing so, feeling like a hero. A hero? At least to myself. I've always done it.

But something happened—it didn't work this time. Surprise. In fact, shock. What I saw was not a hero's grin. What I saw was a sneer, mocking myself. Now, I tear away from the mirror of water. My breath is ragged with fear.

Has anyone witnessed the insult? Rosie's not back yet, so no one watched. Maybe only the girl riding her banana raft. But she pretends to be looking at the grill.

What's that hot wetness on my cheeks, at the corners of my mouth, tasting like sea water? What's the water burning my view? Tears? I don't know. Maybe they're tears. Am I crying? Maybe I'm crying, so what? I haven't cried for a long time.

Am I breaking down? Let it be. Maybe I feel like breaking down. I had it long coming. The wetness in the corners of my mouth tastes bitter as hell, so what? A man, yet by this burning water a little boy again, I feel good. Maybe I feel like knowing what a breakdown feels like. I'm not against any new experience. Never been. This trip is the best proof. I'm grateful for the opportunity to taste a breakdown. I'm grateful to Hersh, Carlo and Tip for pushing me *not* to go. I'm grateful to other friends for pushing me to go. Thank God, I'm experiencing a breakdown, a good one at that, not a fake, not chicken shit. A good, crushing breakdown is hard to come by nowadays. I'm an American. No one cries in America. No one cries in the United States of Happiness. No one sobs. No one bursts into tears. "Never let them see you bleed," Hersh says often. His credo. So no one breaks down. One can only get "stressed"—a shrink can fix it. No biggies. So no one can get a good, degrading, old-fashioned breakdown in America.

Luckily, I came here. Thank God I'm here. Thank God for Mexico. I'm eternally grateful for the opportunity to have a fucking honest breakdown somewhere in the world. I've been looking for it everywhere, checking out all the wrong places but, finally, I got it. I got it. Thank God.

I open my eyes and look around to make sure no one's looking.

Now, I wish I could close my eyes forever. Right across the pool, facing me, I see a big guy who looks like Polo. Is it him? If not, it sure is his spitting image—the same mountain of muscles,the same pectorals that make his cross look like a golden coin between two pigs. Is it him? The acid-green bandana and Playboy sunglasses change his face. Besides, I've never seen Polo half-naked.

He lies in his pool chair, seemingly asleep, but he watches me from behind his mirrors, flexing his chest muscles. He wasn't here before. But the whole thing, the possibility that he saw me weep, makes me jump into the pool.

When I surface, the beefcake is gone. Was he there at all?

"What's up?" I hear Rosie's voice. She is standing by the pool, her body blooming a pink bikini. She's stretching it over her breasts and buttocks. It doesn't work. It's like trying to wrap a watermelon in a church handkerchief.

"What's going on here, Rosie? Where the hell have you been for such a long time?"

"I need a break from you from time to time, my old man. I need some excitement in my life."

"You've just missed it."

"Don't tell me that."

"You wouldn't believe who I saw just a moment ago."

"A devil?"

"I saw a big, whopping mountain of beef, the kind you love."

Rosie stifles a yawn.

"Don't you believe me?"

"I do."

"Isn't it interesting, why not say extraordinary, to see these beefcakes all over Mexico?"

Rosie stifles another yawn.

"You're obsessed with him."

We get into the Jeep, and I barrel down the cobbled streets of adobes hiding behind walled gardens. In the gardens fig trees mother sweet, meaty figs. Shriveled in the sun, smoked in the traffic gases, the baby figs are caked with road dust. The trees reach over the glass-crowned walls, asking us to help ourselves to their sweet burnt-clay fruit.

"Just passed Aguas," Rosie says.

"Who told you?"

"I read the map."

We exit the *pueblo* and speed down the road, kicking up clouds of dust. I see the sun bake the earth, the apples fall from their trees into the hard-baked dirt. In the oven of the day, Rosie's heart has turned to stone.

There's another *pueblo* without a sign that resembles a pile of skulls and bones.

"We're in the State of Guerrero, I read."

Read your ass.

Right before they die, the sick suddenly get well, cheer up for some reason, raising hopes. They see what we don't. "So sunny today!" my mother said that night. We jumped. Rosie and I may be at that point.

I have always thought of the palm trees as chlorophyll fountains. I get a kick from looking at them and Rosie does, too. We see them more and more. We catch glimpses of the Pacific.

With the sight of palm trees our spirits zoom upward. The fronds' shadows finger the road, the clouds burst like pillows, and the sky's blue like a baby's bunting. The State of Guerrero counts not—the United States of Happiness does.

The trip is almost over. In two, maybe three hours, we'll be in Acapulco—too late for the cliff-divers, that's true, but never, never too late for the beach and some serious skinny-dipping before returning the Jeep and taking off for Tijuana.

At the first beach I stop, wrap the wheel with a towel, and fall on the sand, throwing my shoes off. My socks smell like a dishrag on fire. Rosie wipes the sweat from between her breasts under her T-shirt, licks her fingers, and spits.

"We're the only people here."

"The first people."

"The nicest thing to do would be to take off all these fig leaves, you know?"

"God's my witness."

I throw off my shirt, then my pants. Rosie bursts out laughing and throws off her T-shirt. I feel her flesh with my slimy hands, and kiss her clammy breasts. Salt, woman, mixed with the hot reek of Poison. We wash with the wine, lick our armpits, crotches, laughing mouths, and fuck like two dogs. Again, she locks my head between her thighs and tries to swallow the snake whole. We wallow in the dirt and grab fistfuls of ooze to goo each other's body from head to toes. We look like mud devils. Rosie is still a balanced diet, and Epiphany was right, "*Poco veneno no mata.*" I make her come with violent stabs, then fall unconscious, exhausted from working the wheel, stepping on the brakes, slapping the Jeep back in gear, watching out for waddling cows, and keeping my eyes on the road up and down through the Sierra Madre del Sur and from thinking *de revolutionibus orbium coelestium* the whole time.

I see a machete thrust into my heart. It's a death blow, I know, so I wake up before I die, before the machete wedges between my ribs, before I hear the crunch of the steel against my backbone. I lie awake. I have seen my death.

Thank you, God. In your goodness you teach us to die, you offer a step-by-step instruction on how to depart, you put us through some little deaths first, so we get the hang of it.

Looking back, how gently I'm being coached into submission, into giving up my illusions of endless living. How sweetly it goes. I'm being coached with enormous patience and understanding. I know how pigheaded I can be. I refuse the hardest of evidence if I get that way. Yet here, I'm talked out of immortality just like that.

God, you have a way with people like me. *"Je suis reduit a l'etat de squelette,"* Arthur Rimbaud wrote from his hospital bed, and I remember Auschwitz. You have a way with those wishing to be immortal—you make them beg to die. You'll make me beg, too. But I know this: When the time comes, I'll be the only bone in the Valley of the Bones that will turn down rising from the dead.

Rosie sleeps with her mouth open. A fly walks a fresh bite on her lower lip but her lips are so dried, burned, and swollen that she has lost any ability to feel. Is it my bite? I don't know. I wave the fly away.

Rosie wakes up right in time for the sunset. Sucking mangos naked, we watch the barn-brush paint job.

"I can't believe I'm here," Rosie says, making sucking noises. She likes mangos for once. "I hate to get impressed with anything but here, in Mexico, there are moments that I can't believe it's really happening to me. Maybe you'll write a book and I'll read in it: *Romeo and*

Juliet, not their real names, stayed at the cute Hotel Excelsior, their luxury suite complete with a hair-drier, walking places, meeting beautiful people, jeeping around, eating tacos, knocking back rounds of tequila, sipping coffees, devouring fruits and screwing up a storm. Juliet had flown in from a snowbound country and now, just hours later, she was in paradise. 'I can't believe I'm here,' she kept saying to herself. 'I can't believe I'm here.'"

"Do you recall the bookends in Mexico City?"

"Why?"

"There isn't a reason in the world why two people shouldn't get a book between them."

"If yes, why not?"

"You can write it!"

"No, I got no talent."

" 'No, I got no talent,' she said, and he took her in his arms and kissed her tenderly."

"Don't say that!"

"Why say, 'Don't say that!' whenever you want something?"

"Not to jinx."

"What's to do?"

"Keep your mouth shut about what you want and talk about what you don't want," Rosie says, throwing her wig off and stepping into the wash of the surf. She wears nothing but her sweethearts. Her clothes lie in stagnant coils.

A lasso of sea onion ties Rosie's thighs. She stretches

her arms up, high above her bald head, waves reaching up her bare, fiery thighs. She gets up on her toes each time a wave wallows by. She stares at the line where the soft sea makes a hard edge. What is in her head? Suddenly she's all cheer. How can she be? The relationship is dead. I feel like sitting *shiva*.

I watch the watermelon clouds. Everything grows big here—trees, clouds, cockroaches—but so do we. Our downs hit the rock bottom and our highs hit the sky. I cheer up, too.

33

An arm snakes around my neck from behind. I wake up but I don't move. Too tired. My hands, my legs are heavy. My back aches for rest, but my mind's up. Working. Registering impulses from outside: the bayfront boulevard traffic—belching diesel fumes, even now at two A.M.— and the dead fish and seaweed smell. So it's Acapulco, no doubt. Now I remember.

We've just arrived, an hour ago. We stumbled upon Hornos Beach, right downtown. Why do they call it Playa Hornos, the Beach of the Ovens? Did the Aztec potters have their stalls here long ago? We came to Hornos Beach to drink tequila, to skinny-dip, to celebrate. First, we went in together. The water was warm. Can you get pregnant skinny-dipping close? I wonder. Now, Rosie's gone to bathe by herself, leaving me here, in a wooden fishing boat sunk in the sand under the *palapas*, a kind of palm-thatched sunshade, to guard our belongings.

I spotted a gang nearby. I watched them watch me watch them. Rosie keeps attracting fans who step on our heels wherever we go—Polo was just one of them. The other kibitzers stay in the dark waiting for the old man to close his eyes. Rosie is back now, grabbing me from behind by the neck. Unmistakably Rosie.

I'm too tired to open my eyes. Too damn tired. For good reason, too. I've been working like a dog in this heat for two days now. First, Mexico City, the Excelsior Hotel, the market trips. Then, shlepping up the serpentine to Cuernavaca and Taxco, then downhill, all the way to the sea. Finally, Acapulco. I keep my eyes closed. If I did open them, I would see Rosie's head, without being able to see her features, against a bunch of stars, shooting down through the fronds. But I don't have any strength to open my eyes. Just tired. Damn, damn tired. I feel far away, weak, dizzy and woozy. I feel my mind losing itself, reeling, then coming back.

Unmistakably Rosie, a cocky poetess. What's with her? Soft and nice-smelling, her arms spell bliss, no matter what. It's Acapulco, after all, the tourist's paradise, the top of fancies and dreams. Is it strange, a girl getting "sticky?"

One has to understand that. In my letters, I'd been telling Rosie, over and over again, that I'd help her out of Poland. She couldn't stand it there. I understood that. I'd been there. The police began following her wherever she went. I'd been followed, too. So I said I'd help her, and I did. Your word's your word. Our meeting at the Mexico City airport was a howler. So she's happy. Besides, I kept repeating: "We'll be in Acapulco," and now, we *are* in Acapulco. No shit. The word's the word.

Macho stuff. So Rosie's hot. Getting sticky. She wants attention. She might even want to screw, right here and right now, in the boat, despite the fact that I'm dog-tired. Despite the clashes we've gone through.

Make love? Right here? On the beach? At two A.M.? Of course, why not? Great idea. After all, the Mexican police are asleep in their cars—we saw them while walking from the parking lot along the oceanfront.

Each time Rosie feels like making out she walks up to me from behind, hiding her face. Just like now. She gets behind my back, unexpectedly, slyly and, pretending it's not a big deal, she plays with my beard, tickles me, breathes into my ear, or simply warms my back with her boobs. I love all of it.

But this time it is somehow different. The hold on my neck is getting tight. Her soft arm is not soft. I feel hard muscles.

It's not Rosie's arm. Not her sweet flesh. Not a hug, damn it. It's a grip. A vulgar nelson. Deceitful, piggish number, one I haven't by God expected. I stretch my mouth, goggle my eyes, try to howl, but all I'm giving out is a death rattle. Someone is strangling me.

I can't catch my breath. The air is warm and thick. It seems I need two breaths to get a lungful of air. Now, I can't catch a breath at all. I'm nailed to the side of the boat with the bulk of the bull who is strangling me. I hear bare feet padding in the sand.

A few minutes ago a gang of seven, maybe eight

barefooted kibitzers walked by, pretending not to notice me. In turn, of course, I pretended not to notice them. I kept watching them, though. I recall the soles of their feet—the white soles of people who never wore shoes— and their deep-fried backs, some showing through tattered T-shirts. Their backs, that's all I saw. Now, I see their fronts against the stars—the unknown stars of the tropical sky. They rush from all sides, rifling my luggage. My God, a machete.

I have had a few close calls. Once I almost landed on Abraham's bosom. An accident. But never has my life hung on the thrust of a machete pointed at my heart. Especially at the end of a hard, long wait. For months I've written hundreds of letters, bullshitted, cajoled, promised coconuts. Finally, my words came true, everything worked out, and now—what an end!

I try to bolt from the boat but all I do is kick the air. It's as if I'm nailed to the wood. The one with the machete keeps me at the tip of the steel. The tip sinks into my flesh and I feel a burning pain. One thrust of the steel and I'm gone. But I don't feel the machete's cold inside my ribcage. The night—black as it is—has some spots that are still darker. Those flash through my mind as my body jerks from the blows of fists.

All things belonging to Rosie and me, one after another, vanish. There goes my Pierre Cardin jacket. With it, all my travel cash. My passport, too. Forty years of being no one, and now I am no one again. When I received my American passport I jumped for joy, I remember. I was somebody, a human again, even being a *shlimazel*. Now, all's lost. There, Rosie's buff-colored bag disappears with her Polish passport and return ticket. Each hand grabs something else. Shifting my eyes from side to side, I'm watching it.

I'm about to die, the certainty no one can share with anyone else, but I don't care. I have to get them back, the passports. We'll be zeros without them. I can't let it happen. It is not a thought; it's an impulse. I shake off the hands that grip me. I feel my muscles flex, tremble. Fireworks. Unexpected. Red, white and blue lights shoot through the dark. I feel pain coming from my eye, my mouth, my right ear. Blows land like gunshots—bang, bang, bang. There's a difference in the sounds the fists make hitting bone and flesh. My face gives out a juicy sound. I hear a crunch as one fist hits my mouth. Are my teeth gone?

I kick blindly. The fireworks go on. It's the Fourth of July under my cranial vault. A vulgar boxing match, a gang against one. There is a word for it—softening. Still, I don't feel the machete inside my ribs. The blood tastes like sea water in my mouth. So this is what my end is going to be like. A shameful end. Spared nothing. Nothing but the future.

I burst into tears, begging for life, but all I hear is a squeal—like that of a slaughtered pig—and a baby's babble, coming from my mouth in turns.

I am catching my breath. The arm that was holding me lets go of my throat. I'm alive. *What am I going to say?* It is the first thought that hits me.

"What are you?" Rosie will puff her lips. "Wimp, or what? You sat there in the boat, picking the lint from your *pupik*, while they were taking it all—passports, cameras, bags, clothes—stripping us bare? That's the man you are? That's a macho? Wimp! Weakling!"

The imprint of a stinking paw still burns my lips. I touch the teeth that seem loose. Two of them stay in my hand, foamed by saliva mixed with blood. I slip them into my hip pocket—who knows, maybe a California dentist can put them back.

Still I can't believe what's happened to me. I could have been dead by now, but I am alive. They didn't stab me. Left me *alive*, pigs. Left me to rot in shame. What's to be expected? Whatever is unmistakably piggish, it's exclusively human. God, what a shitpile I fell into, what shame. No matter how I juggle the facts, how I handle the angles, what airs I assume, I'll look like a chickenheart, not a macho. Can't come up smelling like a rose. How to live in such shame?

"God, undo the thing!" I lisp. "Don't let it be truth!" I whimper, hobbling toward the sea to tell Rosie, forgetting that the only thing God can't do is to undo what's done. In the sounds I make I can't recognize myself. Without teeth, one makes weird sounds, spits all over one's chin, whimpers weakly.

Where are they?

They ran away under the *palapas* along the beach just outside the bright lights of the promenade. I hear nothing but the traffic. Without shirts, without shoes, they faded out.

Who have they robbed? A Rothschild? A Rockefeller? They robbed the kind of a have-not they are themselves. Manhattan white trash. One thousand bucks. One thousand hours in front of the hissing oven. All gone.

I can feel the heat belching as I fling open the iron door to take out the baked pies. The telephones ring off the hook, all four of them, Joy and I take turns taking orders, the gas is hissing, the oven is humming, radiating hellish heat. The ingredients spoil quickly, smell bad; pizzas bake fast, burn fast, too, if not rushed out; people walk in, pay, walk out, walk in again; the heavy metal coming through the loudspeakers rocks the walls, making it hard at times to understand what the caller wants. My English is still shaky, but I want to speak it, hear it right. I want to know whether it was "crest" or "breast," "not half-done" or "got hard bone." The delivery bikers burst in, pick up the pies, burst out. Spinning a pie is the only moment I can look away from the dough, green peppers, red peppers, pepperoni, apple, pineapple, mushrooms, anchovies, onions, olives, all that. The heat sears my hands, parches my face. Never before have I seen wrinkles forming on my face as fast as now. I age like a dog.

True, the rich do come to Acapulco, but one can't see them. They don't drive Jeeps. They don't skinny-dip on the public beaches at night. They don't meet the street people. They stay far enough away for the stink to smell romantic, and high enough for the poverty to look picturesque. They lounge by the sky-high pools of the luxury hotels, unapproachable, untouchable, unperturbed, money no object, leaving big tips, and it's only us—homeless, beaten, kicked and stoned dogs, scurrying everywhere for scraps of food and constantly threatened in our existence—who jump on each other's throats, fighting for a bone thrown between us. We poor, scabby, starved curs.

34

Rosie's breasts shine in the dark like potbellied pitchers bursting with milk. She noticed nothing, heard nothing, knows nothing of what has just happened. I spit it all out.

"You're kidding," she says.

"Let's go!" I yell at the top of my voice. "We got to call the police!" I grab her by her elbow, pull her against me, cover her with my body, and drag her toward the oceanfront boulevard.

"My clothes?"

"There's no clothes."

"Passports?"

"There's no passports. There's no clothes. There's nothing!" I scream, dragging her into the light. The promenade is as bright as day.

Rosie hides behind a palm tree, crying. I'm mad as hell. She won't come out naked.

I haven't seen her crying since the night when she missed her train. It felt great to have a man follow her throughout Mexico, getting ready to snatch her, carry her away in his arms from her old man to the happy ending. What he snatched, however, was not her but an armful of her clothes, cheap *shmattes* to be cashed in at a flea market. She cries from shame.

"Taxi?" I hear from all sides. "Taxi?"

These yokels would love to give us a ride. They'd take a roundabout way, circle around a lousy *zócalo* several times, and let us off a block from here, asking a bandit's fee. I know you, goons. Rip-off artists. Bloodsuckers. Robbers. I don't have a cent now. You yokels, or sons of bitches like you, relieved us of all our cash.

"Fuck off," I yell back in the face of the most insistent ones. I circle Rosie's palm tree, watching for a cop car. The cabbies, the tourists wonder, what's the loco gringo doing? Barefooted? What's wrong with him? Half-naked, why? Stepping into the soot-belching traffic? Mindless of the yahoos?

Are there any police patrolling the streets? If there were, there're none now. I can't leave Rosie alone while I go to wake up the squad in the back alley.

I see a young man walking the other side of the boulevard. He is carrying something that looks like a woman's purse.

"*¡Perdóne me!*" I call him, jumping between the zooming cars.

The man recognizes me, his eyes grow to the size of watermelons and he quickens his pace, stealing side glances.

"He's got my purse!" Rosie shrieks from behind the palm tree.

I thrash through the orchids growing on the divider and rush between the cars going the other way. Brakes whimper, wheels squeal, rubber burns, drivers growl curses. I don't care. I run, yelling, "Thief! Thief!" The man turns a corner. I turn the corner right after him. But where is he? There's no one around the corner. He has vanished.

"Taxi?" I hear behind me. To hell with you thieves, to hell with you all. I'm getting furious. "Taxi?" I hear the voice again. Another thief who has no idea that the previous thief left me naked. But the cabbie stands, waiting. "Taxi?"

"Police!" I yell in his face but he invites me inside. I call Rosie across the street. I still can't believe it.

"We've been robbed on the beach," I tell him. I know that every cabbie speaks English. "Got no cash! Zip. Zero. Zilch!"

The cabbie's silence is full of understanding. He makes a U-turn, invites Rosie inside. He waits, looking at the rear mirror. I get off, embrace her, and slip her into the back seat, covering her with my arms.

"We lost everything," I tell the taxidriver, but he says nothing. He drives with a steady hand. He seems proud of his Ford—the type still seen in the United States only in car cemeteries. He watches Rosie as if taking her measure for a new bikini. He drives along the promenade as if he needs the bright lights, never taking his eyes off her. The taxi driver has bushy eyebrows, grown together at the base of his nose, reminding me of Epiphany, the Mexican I nicknamed "Funny" during my flight. "Don't lose my phone number," she said. But I did. I'll never see her again. I don't need to. I hug Rosie tighter.

Just in case, I check the dashboard for the driver's name or his business number. There're none. No identification. Instead, I see shmaltzy, filthy, dog-eared pictures of saints glued to the odometer. The odometer is dead.

The taxi turns into a back alley.

"Where the hell are you going?" I yell at the driver. I call him yokel, blockhead, son of a bitch, and grab Rosie's hand, getting ready to jump off.

The taxi stops in front of a small adobe under big-branched fig trees like I've never seen before. The adobe looks like a ruin. We pull over next to two cars with California license plates.

The cabbie whistles.

A young woman pops her head over a balcony, wrapping herself in a man's jacket. Her bulging boobs show bare. Through the door behind her come the voices of *norteamericanos*, the clinking of glasses. Who's this girl? Looks familiar.

The driver and the young woman whisper. The woman disappears. Then she comes back, holding a bundle in her hands. The driver catches the bundle in the air, hands it to Rosie, and burns rubber.

"Where're we going now?" Rosie asks.

"Police, please," I tell the driver. The man says nothing. He acts deaf but drives back to the bayfront boulevard.

Rosie throws me a shirt.

In the boulevard lights the shirt looks like the shirt Stew wore—a tobacco-yellow Calvin Klein polo. Baggy, too. Stew's shirt. Is Stew dead? That house was not the house of the dead. That's obvious. What girl made Stew take off his polo? I throw the shirt on.

Rosie holds a pair of Levi's and a sweatshirt. Hiding behind the seat she slithers into her new clothes, then faces me, all smiles.

It kills me.

Her sweatshirt reads *The Bottomless Pit Bible College*. No wonder the girl on the balcony looked familiar.

The U.S. consul pulled over in front of the police station at four A.M. He offered a loan for two bus tickets to Mexico City. I signed the papers. He said he'd wait at the Tres Estrellas de Oro bus terminal at six A.M. with the tickets.

The Mexican police make no offer of help. There's no sympathy for us. Just the contrary—Rosie and I have become the station's laughingstock. The guys look happy about what happened to us. I think I understand. It's the festering envy of people devoid of opportunity. I understand my attackers, too. I feel for them. Before they attacked me, in their thinking I had it all, and they had nothing. Now, they got it all, and I got nothing. The difference between us, however, is the difference between up and down. Soon, they'll have nothing again. They'll spend it all and they'll have zilch, as always, because in order to have it all one has to have opportunity, and they were born without one. We're different have-nots.

"Please accept my invitation to a small breakfast at the terminal," the consul says, rolling up the window of his Continental as he leaves the police station parking lot.

"Where are we going?" Rosie asks.

"Anywhere."

We end up on Hornos Beach, exactly where I was attacked. The night has entered its darkest core but the starlight outlines everything. Besides, the boulevard bustles nearby. Here, I was dozing. Here, against the boat's side I rested my back, and there, to be exact, under the bench as well as on the top of it, all our belongings had been. Something has drawn us back here.

We climb into the boat, its bow driven deep in the sand, and sit at opposite ends.

I lift my shirt to check the machete wound in the light of the boulevard. A few meat flies start to orbit my rib cage.

"The wound looks like a rosebud," Rosie says.

"It's rotting."

Rosie chortles.

"It'll heal by your wedding day, sweetie."

"I'm rotting, though."

"You're alive."

"Rotting alive."

"You wouldn't bloom in a tomb," Rosie says. "Only live flesh blooms with wounds."

"In Acapulco, the prettiest place to die."

Rosie strips off her clothes.

"Wanna skinny-dip one more time?" she says, running toward the water.

I don't feel any fear any more. I don't know if it was

fear I felt before but if it was, I don't feel it now. I have no fear of losing anything. That's how it feels. It's the realization I no longer have anything to lose. I feel naked.

I lean back against the edge of the boat, gripping its sides. My hands touch splinters. The wood cuts into my back, a nail freezes the small of my back. I feel sweat trickling down my armpits. My lips and cheeks are swollen, but they're healing.

There's no tension anywhere in my flesh. For the first time I see what tension I kept in those little face muscles, maintaining my winning smile. The swelling makes it impossible to flex any muscles. I lean over the boat's side to splash some cold water on the swelling and to check my face. All I see is the globe of my head.

I feel I've lost my face, lost it forever, and I feel free of it. Empty, rather. I feel empty because I don't care any more. I don't care about trying to save face—it's lost, lost forever. Lost with everything else. There's nothing left. There's nothing to be saved and, by some survival instinct buried in my ego, I'm cutting myself free from the loss.

Something about it feels good. What's that? Go figure. Slowly, I'm getting it. It's a shock. This is not my last loss. Now, I know I can get rid of everything that's worthless, everything that's not me. I know how to free myself from any pretense. There's no face to defend, guard, save anymore. They all go. In fact, the more faces I lose the better. The face I lose is not me. I'm not lost. I'll never be lost. There's only face to be lost. I've got many of them, layers and layers of faces to lose. Now, I know that to be is to lose. I accept loss forever.

An arm snakes around my neck from behind. I bolt upright as though touched by a live wire.

It's Rosie's arm, not the robber's. Sweet girl, she's innocent. She beams an apology. The experience has fixed itself already in my mind. She knows.

"I'm going to lie down now," she says, lying against my wound. "Life's a bitch."

We make love, holding back nothing. We are through with caution. We're in danger of nothing. That's it. What can we lose? Everything's lost. If you get into shit like that, you realize all you got is the moment. We pulse wildly in the mud. That's the end. There's nothing in the whole damn world that's more beautiful than love, so we got it all. That's all we need. Money buys everything but love. You love, or you don't. We do, at least at this moment. We love each other, drunk on loss. At this beach, the place where we lost everything money can buy, we celebrate getting out of the gunk naked.

Love is what you want, strive for, can't live without, but can't have—not in the real sense. Why? It's a feeling, actually not one. It's a rush. Can't have it. Can only find yourself for a moment possessed of whatever that is—Bliss? Ecstasy? Rapture? Coming unglued? Falling into pieces? Call it paradise, call it this, call it that, whatever. That's all that is. That's all God's given us. It comes once, maybe twice in a life time—if at all. It makes you coco loco.

I wait for the sun to rise, concentrating on the bloody slot between sky and earth. Now, the sun is up. There was no sunrise. The sun doesn't rise here, it pops up, like a blood-soaked heart born from the breast of the earth.

Rosie and I walk across Papagayo Park to the Tres Estrellas de Oro bus terminal. In Mexico City, we'll approach our respective embassies to issue us new passports.

So I didn't get her over to America. Or, did I? Mexico is America. I used to promise her a palm-fringed paradise. We're in one. We didn't live in it for long, but so what? Who said we should? The lifetime turned out to be a day. The high and the low encompassed by the blink of an eye.

The park gate looks like a mouth about to swallow us whole. We walk toward it under huge fig trees, their branches joined above our heads. The perfumes of eternal spring mix with the rude odor of burning trash. Every new day starts with burning the rot.

Reaching the gate, we see a bonfire of dry fronds, broken tree limbs, rotten fruit, dead leaves, pizza boxes, glass shards, clay shells, soiled clothes, and old newspapers used as toilet tissue. The gardener, the god Tlaloc alive in his burnt-clay features, rakes the fire with a big poker. He wears blue overalls and a big sombrero with holes eaten away by his sweat. We watch him watching us watching him.

As we pass the gate, looking at him, he lifts a brand plucked from the fire into the air, and holds it high.